The Island of the Stairs

Cyrus Townsend Brady

Illustrated by the Kinneys

ESPRIOS DIGITAL PUBLISHING

The Island of the Stairs

Cyrus Townsend Brady

THE ISLAND OF THE STAIRS

THE FLIGHT FROM THE PLACE OF HORROR

The Island of the Stairs

By CYRUS TOWNSEND BRADY

Author of "The Island of Regeneration," "As the Sparks Fly Upward," "The West Wind," Etc.

With Four Illustrations By
THE KINNEYS

A. L. BURT COMPANY, PUBLISHERS
114-120 East Twenty-third Street - - New York
PUBLISHED BY ARRANGEMENT WITH A. C. McCLURG & COMPANY

The
Island of the Stairs

By CYRUS TOWNSEND BRADY
Author of "The Island of Regeneration," "As the Sparks Fly Upward," "The West Wind," Etc.

With Four Illustrations By
THE KINNEYS

A. L BURT COMPANY, PUBLISHERS
114-120 East Twenty-third Street - - New York
PUBLISHED BY ARRANGEMENT WITH A. C. MCCLURG & COMPANY

COPYRIGHT
A. C. McCLURG & CO.
1913
Published November, 1913
Copyrighted in Great Britain

*This story is affectionately
dedicated to my far-off adventurous
Brother-in-law,*

E. S. BARRETT

EDITOR'S NOTE

In order to safeguard the reputation of that worthy seaman and most gallant gentleman who writes this memoir, the editor thereof deems it proper to call attention to the fact that Master Hampdon has described accurately the Island of Mangaia of the Cook, or Hervey, group in the South Seas. It is still completely encircled by the unbroken barrier reef, over which the natives ride in their light canoes. The stairs still exist despite the earthquake to which Master Hampdon refers—and other upheavals which may have followed—and are still traversed by the feet of curious, if infrequent, visitors. For the rest, such altars and platforms as he and his little lady found still abound in the South Seas. Also on Easter Island, and on others, too, such statues of the grotesque and hideous "Stone Goddes" as he describes may be seen. Who made them and why, as well as when they were put there, are as much mysteries today as they were when, in that far-off time, Master Hampdon and his lady sailed those then unknown seas in that brave little barque *The Rose of Devon*.

C. T. B.

Mount Vernon, N. Y.

ILLUSTRATIONS

The flight from the place of horror *Frontispiece*

"The treasure is thereabouts"

Then she bent over me

She had stepped out by my side

The Island of the Stairs

BOOK I

WITHIN THE CASTLE WALLS

The Bequest of the Old Buccaneer

CHAPTER I
WHEREIN I BAIT THE LIVING OVER THE DEAD

I CANNOT say that I was greatly surprised when I stumbled across the body of Sir Geoffrey in the spinney, which is not for a moment meant to convey the impression that I was not shocked. Many times before that morning in my long and adventurous life I had, as I have often since, seen many people die in all sorts of sudden and dreadful ways, in all parts of the globe, too. And in some cases where the sufferer was past hope and the suffering great, I have prayed for the good mercy of a quick end; but never, even under such circumstances, have I been able to look upon death philosophically, at least afterwards. The shock is always there. It always will be, I imagine; indeed I would not have it otherwise. I hope never to be indifferent to the passing of that strange mysterious thing we call life. But I digress.

Truth to tell, I had expected that Sir Geoffrey would come to some such sad end, therefore, I repeat that I was not surprised; but as I stood over him in the gray dawn, looking down upon him lying so quietly on his back with the handsome, silver-mounted, ivory-handled dueling pistol, with which he had killed himself, still clasped in his right hand, I was fascinated with horror. I was younger then and not so accustomed to sudden death as I have become since so many years and so much hard service have passed over my head.

And this was in a large measure a personal loss. At least I felt it so for Mistress Lucy's sake, and for my own, too. Sir Geoffrey had been my ideal of the fine gentleman of his time. I liked him much. He had

The Island of the Stairs

often honored me with notice and generally spoke me fair and pleasantly.

In his situation some men would have blown out their brains—and there would have been a singular appositeness in the action in his case—but Sir Geoffrey had carefully put his bullet through his heart. It was less disfiguring and brutal, less hard on those left behind, less troublesome, more gentlemanly! I divined that was his thought. He was ever considerate in small matters.

The red stain that had welled over the fine ruffled linen, otherwise spotless, of his shirt and the powder marks and burns still visible thereon in spite of the dried blood, all indicated clearly what had happened. The pistol was a short one, heavy in build, made for close work, else he could never have used it so effectively. For the rest, he was clad in his richest and best apparel. His sword lay underneath him, the diamond-studded hilt protruding. He must have fallen lightly, gently, I thought, because his body lay easily on its back and his dress was not greatly disturbed.

I guessed that he was glad enough, after all, that the end had come, for his countenance had not that look of pain, or horror, or fear upon it, which I have so often seen on the face of the dead. His features were calm and composed. Evidently he had not been dead long. I remember the first thing I did was to reach down and gently close his eyes. I shall never forget them to my dying day. They were dreadfully staring. As I bent over him for this purpose I noticed that he had something in his left hand. That hand was resting lightly by the hilt of his sword as if he had stood with his left hand on his sword in that gallant defiant position which I had often enough seen him assume, when he pressed the trigger with his right hand. As he had fallen, his hand had been lifted a little away from the sword and in his fingers there was a paper. A nearer look showed it to be an envelope. I drew it away and, glancing at it, saw that it was addressed to Mistress Lucy. Thrusting it in the pocket of my coat, I rose to my feet.

At that instant I heard steps and voices. Now I had nothing on earth to fear from anybody. The death of Sir Geoffrey was too obviously a suicide for anyone to accuse me, even if there had been any reason whatever for bringing me under suspicion. The letter which I carried in my pocket addressed to Mistress Lucy would undoubtedly explain everything there was to explain. Something, however, moved me to seek concealment. I am a sailor, as you will find out, and act quickly in an emergency by a sort of instinct. On the sea men have little time for reflection. The crisis is frequently upon one with little or no warning, and generally it must needs be met on the instant and without deliberation.

Sir Geoffrey lay on the side of the path which ran through the spinney and beyond him the coppice thickened. The path twisted and turned. From the sound of the footsteps, I judged that men were coming along it. I instantly stepped across the body and concealed myself behind a tree trunk in the leafy foliage of the undergrowth. I could see without being seen, and hear as well.

The approaching footsteps might belong to some of the gamekeepers, to a stray poacher, to some of the servants of the castle, or to someone who, like myself, had been abroad in the gray dawn and had been attracted to the spot by the sound of the shot, although they approached over leisurely for that. I was prepared for any of these things but I did not expect that any of the guests of the castle would make their appearance at that hour. The footsteps stopped. Two men, one of whom had been pointed out to me as Baron Luftdon in the lead followed by another who was strange to me, suddenly appeared. A voice which I recognized as the baron's at once exclaimed in awe-struck tones:

"By gad, he's done it!"

"Yes," drawled the other, whose cold blooded calmness was in marked contrast with the unwonted excitement of the first speaker, "I rather expected it."

"Here's a pretty affair," said the first man.

"Oh, I don't know," said the second indifferently, "it might be worse."

"Worse for him? Great heavens, man, he's dead!"

"Worse for us."

"What d' ye mean? I don't understand."

"Well, for instance, he might have shot himself before we—ah—plucked him."

"Oh, I see," returned my lord with a rather askant glance at his companion, for which I almost respected him for the moment.

The two stepped a little nearer. The first speaker, Lord Luftdon, one of the young bloods who had been having high carouse with Sir Geoffrey for the past week at the castle, bent over him.

"There's no doubt about his being dead, I suppose?" he asked after a brief inspection.

"Good gad, no," replied the second man with a contemptuous laugh. "Where are your wits, man? He must have held the muzzle of the pistol close to his breast. See how his shirt is burned and powder blackened. He must have died instantly."

"I suppose you are right."

"Well," continued the drawler nonchalantly—as for me I hated them both but the latter speaker the more if possible, for reasons which you will presently understand—"this relieves me greatly."

"What do you mean?"

"You are very stupid this morning, *mon ami*," returned the other, gracefully taking a pinch of snuff and laughing again with that horrible indifference to the dead man who had been his host and friend.

"After such a night as we had, to come thus suddenly upon—this—'tis enough to unsettle any man," muttered Luftdon apologetically.

"Pooh, pooh! man, you're nervous."

"Well, I don't know how it relieves you. And after all's said and done, Wilberforce was a gentleman, a good player and a gallant loser, and I liked him."

"Exactly, I liked him too, well enough. And he lost his all like a gentleman."

"And you got it, at least most of it."

"Patience, my friend, you had your share, you know," returned the other with his damnable composure.

"I don't know but I'd give it back to have poor old Geoff with us once again," retorted Luftdon with some heat.

"That is a perfectly foolish statement, my buck," returned the other, philosophically taking snuff. "Somebody was bound to get it; Wilberforce has been going the pace for years; we happened to be in at the death, that's all."

"Well, how does it relieve you, then? Do you think Wilberforce would have attempted to get you to support him?"

The drawler laughed.

"Of course not, this"—he pointed to the dead body—"is proof enough of the spirit that was in him; but of course, I cannot marry the girl now."

"You can't?"

"Certainly not. Her father a bankrupt and a suicide—"

"But the castle and this park?"

"Mortgaged up to the hilt. Speaking of hilts—" he stooped down and daintily avoiding contact with the corpse, drew from the scabbard the diamond-hilted sword—"this belongs to me. It's worth taking. You remember he staked it last night on the last deal."

"Good God, man," protested the first speaker, "don't take the man's sword away. Let him lie with his weapons like a gentleman."

"Tut, tut, you grow scrupulous, it seems. We will provide him a cheaper badge of his knighthood, if necessary," returned the other lightly.

"And about the girl?"

"'Tis all off."

"You will have some trouble breaking your engagement with her, I am thinking."

"Not I. To do her justice, the wench has the spirit of her father. A whisper that I am—er—disinclined to the match will be quite sufficient."

"Aye, but who will give her that whisper?"

"We will arrange that some way. Truth to tell, I am rather tired of the minx, she bores me with her high airs. She does not know that she is penniless and disgraced. And as for her good looks—'tis a country beauty after all."

"Poor girl—" began Luftdon, whose face, though bloated and flushed and seamed with the outward and visible evidences of his evil life, still showed some signs of human kindness.

At that point I intervened. I could bear no more. When they spake so slightingly of my little mistress it was more than I could stand. I burst out of the brush and stood before them—mad, enraged all through me. I will admit that I lacked the composure and breeding of that precious pair. What I had heard had filled me with as hot an indignation as ever possessed the soul of man, and with every moment the fire of my resentment burned higher and more furiously. They started back at my sudden appearance, in some little discomfiture, from which he of the slower speech the more speedily recovered. He was the greater man, and eke the greater villain. The younger, the one with the red face, looked some of the discomposure he felt. The other presently leered at me in a deliberate and well intentioned insulting way and began:

"Now who may you be, my man, and what may you want?"

"Who I may be matters nothing," said I, "but what I want matters a great deal."

"Ah! And what is it that you want that matters so much?"

"In the first place, that sword."

"This?" asked the sneering man, holding Sir Geoffrey's handsome weapon lightly by the blade and smiling contemptuously at me.

"That," answered I with equal scorn.

I am accustomed to move quickly as well as to think quickly, and before he knew it, I had it by the hilt and but that he released the blade instantly I would have cut his hand as I withdrew it. He swung round and clapped his hand on his own sword, a fierce oath breaking from his lips, his face black as a thundercloud.

"Don't draw that little spit of yours," I said, "or I will be under the necessity of breaking your back."

I towered above both of them and I have no doubt that I could have made good my boast. Yet, to do him justice, the man had the courage of his race and station. He faced me undaunted, his hand on his sword hilt.

"Would you rob me of mine own, Sirrah?" he asked more calmly if not less irritatingly.

"I might do so, and with justice," I replied. "You had no hesitation in robbing the living or the dead."

"Zounds!" cried the other man, touched on the raw of a guilty conscience apparently, "'twas in fair play. We risked each what we had and Sir Geoffrey lost."

"Yes, I see," I replied. "Having paid you with everything else, and possessing nothing beside, he had to throw away his life in the end. I heard what you said. You wonder how Mistress Wilberforce is to learn the situation—you who have doubtless once borne the reputation of a man of honor! You wonder who is to tell her that you discard her. I will."

"That is good, well thought of, yokel," said the drawler with amazing assurance, and keeping his temper in a way that increased mine, "I could not have wished it better. As for your reflections upon me they interest me not at all. You are doubtless some servant of the house—"

"I am no man's servant," I interrupted in some heat.

"Somebody born on the place who probably cherishes a peasant's humble admiration for the lady of the manor," he continued.

I displayed the red ensign in my weather-beaten cheeks at this. I never was good at the dissimulation that goes on in polite society and I never could control my color for all I am bronzed with the wind and spray of all the seas, to say nothing of tropic suns.

"Ah," he laughed sneeringly, taking keen note of my confusion, "see the red banner of confession in the brute's face, Lord Luftdon."

"I see it, of course," said the other, whose frowning face was far redder than my own, though from drink—"but I must confess that personally I don't like the allusion."

"That for your likes, Luftdon," cried the other as contemptuous of his companion as of me apparently. "Tell her, my man, tell her. Tell her that she is a beggar and her father a suicide, and that I have all her property without her. She can go to your arms or those of any other she fancies. She is not meet for the Duke of Arcester."

So this was Arcester! I had heard of him, as I had of Luftdon, two of the most debauched, unprincipled rakes, idlers, fortune hunters, gamblers, men-about-town, in all England. But of the two he bore much the worse reputation. Indeed, no one in that day surpassed him in baseness and villainy. But that he was a duke, he had been branded, jailed, or even hanged long since in England. But I cared nothing for his dukedom. As he spoke thus slightingly of my lady, I stepped closer to him and struck him with the palm of my hand. I suppose a gentleman would have tapped him lightly but not being of that degree I struck hard across the face, not so hard as I might have, to be sure, for I could doubtless have killed him, but hard enough to make him reel and stagger. His sword was out on the moment but before he could make a pass I wrenched it from him, broke the blade over my knee and hurled the two pieces into the coppice.

"I can match you with swords," said I, coolly enough now that the issue was made and the battle about to be joined. "I have fought with men, not popinjays, in my day, all over the world, and I know the use of the weapon; but I would not demean myself, being an honest man though no gentleman, much less a duke, by crossing blades with such a ruffian."

"By God!" cried the duke furiously, "I will have you flogged and flung into the mill pond, I will clap you in jail, I will—"

"You will do nothing of the sort," said I, composedly. "There is no man on the estate who would not take my part against you, especially when I repeat what you have said about Mistress Lucy. They love her and they loved him. With all his drink and extravagance he was a good master and you have been a bad friend."

"And who would believe you?" queried the duke, whose anger was at a frightful height in being thus braved and insulted. In his agitation he tore at his neckcloth and almost frothed at the mouth like a man in a fit—I doubt he had ever been so spoken to before. "'Twould be your word against mine, you dog, and—"

"For the matter of that, my word will not be uncorroborated," I interrupted swiftly.

"What d' ye mean, curse you?"

"This gentleman—"

"By gad," said Lord Luftdon, decisively, responding to my appeal more bravely than I had thought, "you are right to appeal to me and you were right to strike Arcester. 'Fore God, I'm sorry for the girl and for Sir Geoffrey and ashamed for my—my—friend."

"Would you turn against me in this?" asked the duke, surprised at this amazing defection.

"I certainly would," answered the other with dogged courage.

"God!" whispered his grace hotly, fumbling at the empty sheath, "I wish I had my sword. I'd run the two of you through!"

"There is Sir Geoffrey's sword," said Lord Luftdon, who did not lack courage, it seemed, clutching his own blade as he spoke and making as if to draw it.

"No," said I, master of the situation as I meant to be, "there shall be no more fighting over the dead body of Sir Geoffrey. You and Lord Luftdon can settle your differences elsewhere. I am glad for his promise to tell the truth in case you attempt to carry out your threat and I am just as grateful as if it had been necessary."

"On second thought, there will be no further settlement," said Luftdon, regaining his coolness and thrusting back into its scabbard his half-drawn blade. "His grace and I are in too many things to make a permanent difference between us possible."

"I thought so," I replied.

"By gad," laughed Luftdon, "I like your spirit, lad. Who are you, what are you?"

"The late gardener's son."

"Do they breed such as you down here in these gardens?"

"As to that, I know not, my lord. I am a sailor. I have commanded my own ship and made my own fortune. I come back here between cruises because I am devoted to—"

"The woman!" sneered the duke, and I marveled at the temerity of the man, seeing that I could have choked him to death with one hand.

"Mention her name again," I cried, "and you will lie beside your victim yonder!"

"Right," said Luftdon approvingly.

"I come back here because I am fond of the old place. Lord Luftdon, it is my home. My people have served the Wilberforces for generations. Their forebears and mine lie together in the churchyard around the hill yonder. You can't understand devotion like that," said I, turning to the duke, "and 'tis not necessary that you should."

"And indeed what is necessary for me, pray?" he sneered.

"That you and Lord Luftdon leave the place at once."

"Without speech with my lady?"

"Without speech with anyone. There is a good inn at the village. I will take it upon myself to see that your servants pack your mails and follow you there at once."

"I will not be ordered about like this," protested the duke blusteringly.

"Oh, yes you will," said Luftdon. "The advice he gives is good. We have nothing more to do here."

"No," said I bitterly, "you have done about all that you can. The man is dead but the woman's heart will not be broke because of you. Now go."

"If I had a weapon," said Arcester slowly, shooting at me a baleful and envenomed glance, "I believe I would even send one of his faithful retainers to accompany Sir Geoffrey."

I never saw a man who was more furiously angry, baffled, humiliated than he. As for me, I was glad of his rage. If I had known any way to make him more angry and humiliated I confess I would have followed it.

"Don't be a fool, Arcester," said the other; "you've got everything you wanted in this game and 'tis only just that you should pay a little for it. What's your name, my man?"

"Never mind what it is."

"Are you ashamed of it?"

"Hampdon!"

"Master Hampdon, you may not be a gentleman," said Luftdon, "but by gad, you are a man, and here's my hand on 't."

He had played a man's part, so I clasped it.

"You will be embracing him next, inviting him to your club, I suppose," said Arcester in mocking contempt.

"No," said Luftdon, sarcastically, "he would not be congenial company for you and me, neither would we be for him. He seems to be an honest man. Let's go."

And so they went down the path, leaving me not greatly relishing my triumph, for now I had to tell Mistress Lucy all that had happened. I had to say the words that would tell of the loss in one fell moment of her father, of her property, and of her lover. I was greatly puzzled what to say and how to say it, for Mistress Lucy Wilberforce was no easy person to deal with at best.

CHAPTER II
WHICH SHOWS HOW I BROKE THE NEWS

THE path from the spinney to the ancient castle which antedated King Henry VIII, and which in its older parts goes much farther back into the past, led through the park full of noble oaks and beeches, many of them older even than the ancient and honorable family which now, alas, bade fair to lose them all forever. As I trudged over it with lagging footsteps, misliking my duty more and more as the necessity for discharging it drew closer, I caught a glint of rapidly moving color on the long driveway that led from the lodge to the steps of the hall. The scarlet of my lady's riding coat as she galloped up the tree bordered road, it was that attracted my attention. I quickened my pace and we arrived at the steps leading up to the terrace at the same instant. She was alone, for she had either chosen to ride unaccompanied, as was her frequent custom, or else, being the better mounted, she had left her groom far behind.

I stood silent before her with that curious dumbness I generally experience—even at this day—when first entering her presence, while she drew rein sharply. She was a little thing compared to me, small compared even to the average woman, but in one sense she was the biggest thing I had ever confronted. No burly shipmaster had ever impressed me so, not even when I was a raw boy on my first cruise. I actually looked upon her with a feeling of—well, shall I say awe?—mingled with other emotions which I would not have breathed to a soul. The chance hit by the Duke of Arcester had brought the color to my cheek and it takes something definite and apposite to bring the color to a bronzed, weather-beaten cheek like mine, which has been thrust into the face of wintry seas and exposed to tropical suns all over the globe. That is the way I thought of her. I was almost afraid of her! I, who feared nothing else on land or sea! What she thought of me was of little moment to her.

It was Mistress Lucy's regular habit to take a morning gallop every day. It was that usual custom that caused her to look so fresh and young and beautiful, that put the color in her cheek and the sparkle in her eye. Although she had left her father playing hard late the night before when she had gone to bed, there had been nothing in that to cause her to intermit her practice. Poor girl, she had left her father doing that more nights than she could remember in her short life, and I suppose she had become used to it, to a certain extent, at any rate.

She nodded carelessly, yet kindly to me. It was her habit, that careless kindness. When she was a little girl and I had been a great boy we had played together familiarly enough—children caring little for distinctions of rank, I have observed—but that habit was long since abandoned. Then she looked about for her groom. The steps that led to the terrace were deserted. Sir Geoffrey of late had grown slack in the administration of affairs on account of his troubles, therefore no attendant was at hand. Like master, like man! I suspected that the servants had kept late hours, too. Indeed they probably plundered Sir Geoffrey in every way and he, seeing that all was gone or going, perhaps shut his eyes to their peculations. They might as well get what was left as his creditors. Mistress Lucy after that first nod stared at me frowning.

"Master Hampdon," she said at last, "since nobody else seems to be about, suppose you attempt the task."

She loosed her little foot from the stirrup and thrust it out toward me. I am nothing of a horseman. I was very early sent off to sea and I have a sailor's awkwardness with horses. Naturally I did not know how a lady should be dismounted from her horse. I had never attempted the thing and I did not recall ever to have seen it done, otherwise I might have managed, for I am quick enough at mechanical things; but her desire was obvious and I must accomplish it the best I could. I stepped over to her, disregarding her outthrust foot, for all its prettiness, seized her about the waist with both hands, lifted her bodily from the saddle and set her down gently on the gravel. She looked at me very queerly and gave a faint shriek when her weight came upon my arms. Indeed, I have no doubt that I held her tightly enough through the air.

"I dare say there is not a man among my father's friends or mine, who could have done that, Master Hampdon," said she, smiling up at me a little and looking flushed and excited.

"'Tis no great feat," said I stupidly enough, "I have lifted bigger—"

"Women!" flashed out Mistress Lucy slightly frowning.

"Things," I replied.

"It amazes me," she said. "I have never been dismounted that way before. However, I remember you always were stronger than most men, even as a boy. There seem to be no grooms about, the place is wretchedly served. Will you take my horse to the stables?" she asked me.

There was a certain flattery to me in that request. If I had not shown her how strong I was, in all probability she would have thrown me the bridle and with a nod toward the stables to indicate her wishes would have left me without a word. Now it was different. I took the bridle, not intending, however, to take the horse around, not because I disdained to do her any service but because I had other duties to discharge more important than the care of horses.

"Have you seen my father this morning?" she asked as I paused before her and then, not giving me time to answer, looked up at the sun. "But of course not," she continued, a little bitterly, "he probably only went to bed an hour or two since and 'tis not his habit to rise so early as you and I."

As luck would have it, while she spoke a sleepy groom chanced to come round the house. I flung the reins to him, bade him take the horse away and turned to my lady.

"Madam," said I, my voice thickening and choking, "as it happens, I have seen your noble father this morning."

There was something in my voice and manner, great stupid fool that I was, that instantly apprised her that something was wrong. With one swift step she was by my side.

"Where?"

"In the spinney."

"When?"

"But just now."

"What does he there at this hour?"

"Nothing."

"I don't understand."

"Sir Geoffrey—" I began racking my brains, utterly at loss what to say next and how to convey the awful tidings.

She made a sudden step or two in my direction, then turned toward the coppice, her suspicions fully aroused.

But now I ventured upon a familiarity, that is, I turned with her and caught her by the arm before she could take a step.

"I will see him myself," she began resolutely.

"Madam," said I swiftly, "you cannot."

"Master Hampdon," she said, "something dreadful has happened."

I nodded.

This was breaking it gently with a vengeance, but what could I do? She always did twist me around her little finger and I was always more or less helpless before her. I admit that. I am still, for that matter, although she will not have it so.

"What is it? Is my father—what is he doing in the spinney? He never rises at this hour."

"Mistress Wilberforce," I said, "you come of a brave stock and the time for your courage is now."

"Is my father dead?" she asked, after a sudden, awful stillness.

I nodded while she stared at me like one possessed.

"Killed in a duel?" she whispered. I shook my head.

"Would to God I could think so," I replied.

"You mean that he was—murdered?"

"Mistress," said I bluntly, seeing no other way, "he died by his own hand."

"Oh, my God!" she cried, clapping her hands to her face and reeling back.

I caught her about the waist. She had no knowledge that she was held or supported, of course; all her interest and attention were elsewhere. She did not weep or give way otherwise. She was a marvelous woman and her self-mastery and control amazed me, for I knew how she had loved her father.

"When? Why?" she gasped out.

"I was early awake and abroad," I answered—and I did not tell her it was my habit to see her gallop off for that morning ride, for even a glimpse of her was worth much to me—"and I heard a shot in the spinney. I hurried there and found Sir Geoffrey—"

"Dead?"

"Stone dead, mistress, with a bullet in his heart."

"Let us go to him."

"No," said I, and I marveled to find myself assuming the direction as if I had been on the deck of my own ship, "that you cannot. It is no sight for your eyes now. I was coming to the castle to tell you and to send the servants to fetch—him. Meanwhile, do you go into the hall and summon your women and—"

"I will do what you say, Master Hampdon," she whispered, very small, very forlorn, very despairing. "My father, oh, my good, kind father!"

She turned, and I still supporting her, we mounted the steps of the terrace. Suddenly she stopped, freed herself, and faced me.

"Lord Luftdon and the Duke of Arcester," she explained, "they are staying at the castle; they must be notified."

"Madam," said I, "they already know it."

"And why then have they left the duty of telling me to you? Where are they? Summon them at once."

"They are gone," I blurted out, all my rage at the duke reviving on the instant.

"Gone!"

"Having won everything from Sir Geoffrey they have left him alone in his death," I retorted bitterly.

"Impossible!"

"I ordered them off the place," I said bluntly.

"You!" she flashed out imperiously. "And who gave you the power to dismiss my—my father's friends?"

"I heard what they said, being close hid myself in the coppice."

"And what said they?"

"It concerned you, mistress."

"The Duke of Arcester," she promptly began, "is my betrothed husband. I will hear no calumny against him."

"Madam," I said, keenly aware that I had made no charges yet and wondering at her thought, "your engagement is broken."

"Broken!" she cried in amaze.

"The duke declared himself to his friend to be too poor to marry the penniless child of a—disgraced man—his words, not mine, believe me."

The awful death of her beloved father had been shock enough to her, but with this insult added I thought she would have swooned dead away. She turned so white and reeled so that I caught her again. I even shook her while I cried roughly,

"You must not give way."

"It is a lie, a dastardly lie!" she panted out at last.

"It is God's truth," said I. "He repudiates you."

"No man could be so base," she persisted, "he swore that he loved me."

"I would it were otherwise, madam, but he is gone, leaving that message for you."

"And he made you his messenger?"

"I volunteered."

"Why? Why?"

"Because he is a low coward."

"And you stood by and let him insult me, your patron's daughter, your mistress?"

Now so far as that went, I had got mightily little out of the late Sir Geoffrey's patronage, but whatever duty I could compass I would gladly pay the little lady who stood before me.

"Mistress, you misjudge me. He had taken Sir Geoffrey's sword, saying that he had won it with everything else. I took it from him. When he said those words about you I struck him across the face, no light blow, I assure you. When he grasped his own sword I wrenched it away from him, broke it, and cast it away. You may find the broken pieces in the spinney. I told him that you were meet for his betters and that you were well rid of him, and bade him begone."

"In that," she said in a certain strained way, "you acted as a loyal servitor of the house and I thank you."

"I am to give orders to have his baggage sent to the inn at once," said I.

"And Lord Luftdon?"

"He came to your defense as if he were still the gentleman he had once been. But he goes hence with his friend. His baggage will also follow him."

"I will attend to that for them both," said Mistress Lucy, growing strangely and firmly resolved again, and even I could guess the tremendous constraint she put upon herself. "Enough of Arcester. I am well rid of him and of his companion. Summon the servants to bring my father's body to the castle. I suppose the crowner will have to be notified."

"Yes," said I. "I will see to that myself."

"Of all my friends," said she piteously, almost giving way, "you seem to be the only one left me, Master Hampdon."

"I have been your faithful servant always, Mistress Lucy," I answered as I ushered her into the hall.

CHAPTER III
IN WHICH I DELIVER A LETTER

I DELIVERED my little mistress to her woman who came at my call, and then I summoned the steward and butler and told them what had happened. In a moment all was confusion. But presently they brought the body of Sir Geoffrey back to the castle which was no longer his. As the duke had said, it was mortgaged to its full value. The unfortunate baronet had gambled away everything in his possession, the family jewels, the heirlooms of his daughter, and even the property that had been left to her by her dead mother, of which he was trustee. Everything that he could get his hands on had been sacrificed to his passion for play.

Following the inquest, and after a due interval to show a decent respect for the dead, there was a great funeral, of course, during which what little ready money there was available was of necessity spent. The gentry came for miles around, even Luftdon was there in the background, although Arcester had the decency to keep away. I was there, too, finding my place among the upper servants of the household. Although I was in no sense a servant of the house, being a free and independent sailorman and my own master, still I found no place else to stand. I was glad that I had taken that position for I happened to be immediately back of Mistress Lucy. From under her veil she shot a forlorn, grateful look at me as she came in, as if she felt I was the only real friend she had in that great assemblage of the gentry of the county and the tenants and dependents of the estate.

Sir Geoffrey, except Mistress Lucy, was the last of his race. The brave, fine old stock had at last been reduced to this one slender slip of a girl. Kith or kin, save of the most distant, she had none. Nor did she enjoy a wide acquaintance. She had never been formally introduced to society. Sir Geoffrey had loved her and had been kind enough to her in his careless, magnificent way, but she had been left much alone since the death of her mother some years before, and she had grown up under the care of a succession of wandering and ill-paid governesses and tutors. The neighboring gentry had assembled for the funeral with much show of sympathy but in my heart I knew that Mistress Lucy felt very much alone and I rather gloried in the position which made me, humble though I was, her friend. Well, she could count upon me to the death, I proudly said to myself. She would find I was always devoted to her and I solemnly consecrated myself anew to her service in her loneliness and bereavement.

The show and parade were over soon enough. The parson's final words of committal were said. We left Sir Geoffrey in his place in the churchyard and went back to the hall, after which the company began to disperse. I had nothing to do at the time. No one paid any attention to me. I held myself above the servants and the gentry held themselves above me. I wandered into the hall and stood waiting. No one spoke to me save Lord Luftdon, who expressed a heart-felt regret that he had had anything to do with the final plundering of the unfortunate baronet, which in a measure had brought about this sorry ending to his career.

"You seem to be a man of sense, Master Hampdon," he whispered, drawing me apart, after it was all over, "and I noticed the way Mistress Wilberforce looked at you when she first came in."

"What do you mean?" I asked hotly, not liking to hear her name on his lips, and especially resenting what I thought was a reflection upon her.

"Nothing but the best," he answered equably. "I have still unspent some of the proceeds of our last bout at the table with her father that could be conveyed to the lady, and—"

"She would burn her hand off rather than accept anything," said I promptly.

"But, man, I wish to—" he persisted.

"It is not to be thought of."

"You speak with authority?" he asked, looking at me strangely.

"I have known her from a child," said I, "and her father before her. It is not in the breed to take favors, and—"

"But this is—er—restitution."

"Did you win it fairly?" I asked.

"By God," he answered, clapping his hand to his sword, "if another had asked me that I would have had him out."

"Your answer?" I persisted, undaunted by his fierceness.

He smiled, his sudden heat dying out apparently as he realized how foolish it was to quarrel with me and discovered the meaning of my question.

"Of course we won it fairly. Sir Geoffrey was the most reckless and even the most foolish gambler I ever played with. We took advantage of that, but there was no cheating, Master Hampdon, no, on my honor, as I am a gentleman."

"Under the circumstances then," said I, "there is nothing further to be said."

"But what will the poor girl do?" he demanded.

I shook my head. I did not know how to answer that question for I did not know what she would do. Nevertheless I was not a little touched and pleased with his interest and desire. Surely the man had some good in him still. Association with such a scoundrel as Arcester had not yet wholly ruined him.

"You should have thought of this before," said I.

"Yes, I suppose so," he admitted rather woefully.

"It is too late to make reparation now, although the wish does you honor, my lord."

"Well, Hampdon, if you have a chance to tell her what I wanted," he said, "please do. I should do it myself," he continued, "only since her repudiation by that blackguard Arcester she will not admit me to speech. By gad—" he looked over at her where she stood in the doorway going through the dreary process of bidding farewell to the guests after the funeral meal that had followed the interment, "by gad, if I were a bit younger and not so confoundedly in debt I would marry the woman myself."

"She is meet for a better man, my lord," said I, exactly as I had answered the duke.

He looked at me curiously for a moment and then laughed loudly.

"Doubtless," he said, "you may tell her that, too."

With that he turned on his heel and walked away and I saw no more of him. I stood idle on the terrace until the last of the gentry had gone. As before, I did not know just what to do or just where to go. My position was most anomalous. I wanted to be of service, but how to offer myself without intrusion, I could not readily discover. It was my lady herself who solved the problem.

"Master Hampdon," she began wearily, "will you come into the house? Master Ficklin, the lawyer, is here, waiting to go over my father's papers with me. You have stood by me manfully, your people and my people have been—" she stopped a moment, "friends," she added with kindly condescension, "for five hundred years. I have no one else with whom to counsel. Come with me."

Sir Geoffrey's will, as Master Ficklin read it, was a simple affair. It left everything of which he died possessed to his daughter. Unfortunately, he died possessed of nothing; the document was mere waste paper. Everything was mortgaged, every family portrait, even. Mistress Lucy appeared to have no legal right to anything in or out of the castle apparently, save the clothes she wore.

"Sir Geoffrey," said Master Ficklin, endeavoring to put a good face on the matter, "was well meaning—most well meaning. Not only did he play high and long at the gaming table but he speculated also, for he was always trusting to recoup himself; in which event doubtless there would have been a handsome patrimony for his daughter."

"You may spare me any encomiums of my father, Master Ficklin," said Mistress Lucy very haughtily; "I knew his devotion and affection better than anyone possibly could."

In her mind there was no double meaning to these brave words she uttered so quickly, although I listened amazed. To rob his daughter of her all in the indulgence of a wicked passion for gaming and speculation was no great evidence of devotion or affection, I thought. However, Master Ficklin was only putting the best face upon a sorry matter, and for that I honored him, for all my mistress' haughty and imperious manner.

The Island of the Stairs

"The point is, however," she continued, as Master Ficklin bowed deferentially toward her, "that I have nothing."

"Nothing from your father, madam," answered the man of law.

"But my mother's estate?"

"I regret to say," said Master Ficklin, "that most of it has been converted into money and—er—lost by your father. Strictly speaking he had no—er—legal right to dispose of your property and we might recover by suits at law from those—"

"I gave him the right," interrupted Mistress Lucy quickly.

She had never given him any such right, of course, but she was jealous for the honor of her father and the family and I could only admire her action, although the plain, blunt truth ever appeals to me, let it hurt whom it may.

"In that case, there is nothing to be said or done," returned the old attorney, who knew the facts as well as I.

"I forget," she went on, "just how much of my mother's property was devoted to—to our needs, by my father and myself."

"There is left in my hands, madam, a matter of some two thousand pounds out at interest which you, being now of full age—"

"I was eighteen on my last birthday."

"Exactly, so that the two thousand is at your present disposal."

"In what shape is it?"

"It is invested in consols."

"Can they be realized upon?"

"Instantly."

"To advantage?"

"Most certainly."

"I thank you, Master Ficklin, for your provident care of my little fortune. It is most unexpected," she faltered, almost overwhelmed at the sudden realization that she was not altogether a pauper.

The Island of the Stairs

"Believe me, Mistress Lucy, it is a happiness to do anything for you," said the old attorney, rising and gathering up his papers, and bowing low before her. "My father, and his father before him served the estates of the Wilberforces, and for how many generations back I know not. You may command me in everything. A temporary loan, or—"

"Thank you, Master Ficklin," said Mistress Lucy, "you touch me greatly, but I need nothing at present. My father made me an allowance and generally paid it. It was a generous one; living alone as I did I could not spend it all. I have a few hundred pounds in my own name at the bank, and with that for temporary use and my mother's legacy I shall lack nothing."

"But where will you live, Mistress Lucy?"

"It matters little," she answered listlessly.

"My sister and I," said the old attorney, "live alone in the county town. The house is large. If you would accept our hospitality until your future is decided we should be vastly honored."

"Master Ficklin—" began my lady.

"I know that the accommodations are poor," interrupted the attorney hastily, "and we are humble folk, but—"

"I accept your kindly proffer most thankfully," was her prompt reply. "I have been invited to various homes here and there in the county, but those who invited me have sought to convey a favor to me by their courtesy and I prefer to go to you."

"Good," said Master Ficklin briskly. "That is settled then. No one has either a legal or a moral claim to your clothes or personal belongings or such jewelry as you have been accustomed to wear or have in your possession. You may pack everything of that sort and take away with you any little keepsake. In fact, I am empowered by those who held the mortgage to tell you that the pictures of your father or mother or anything strictly personal they waive their claim to."

"Thank you," said Mistress Lucy, "I shall take but small advantage of their generosity."

"I know that," answered Master Ficklin, "and now I will return to the town. If you will be ready about six o'clock—" it was then about two—"I will return and fetch you to our home."

"I shall be ready. Good-by."

The little lawyer bent over her hand and left the room. I had sat dumb and silent during the whole interview, although I had listened to everything with the deepest interest. As usual it was she who broke the silence when we were alone again.

"Master Hampdon," she began, "to what a sorry pass am I reduced! What shall I do now?"

"My lady," said I, "the sorriest part of the pass to which you have been brought is that you have in me such a poor counselor, a rough sailor, but one who would, nevertheless, give his heart's blood to promote your welfare, or do you any service."

Now as I said that I laid my hand on the breast of my coat and as I bent awkwardly enough toward her—I could not even bow as gracefully as the little attorney just departed—I felt the paper which I had taken from Sir Geoffrey's hand and which I had entirely forgot in the hurry and confusion of the days that had followed his death. I stood covered with surprise and shame at my careless forgetfulness, and stared at her.

"What is it?" she asked, instantly noting my amaze.

"I am a fool, madam, a blundering fool," said I, drawing forth the paper. "Here is a letter addressed to you which I should have delivered at once," I continued extending it toward her.

"To me? From whom?" she asked.

"Your father."

"My father!" she exclaimed.

"Yes, I took it from his dead hand that morning and thrust it into the breast of my coat and forgot it until this very moment. It may be vital to your future, my carelessness may have lost you—"

"It can lose me nothing," said the girl with unwonted gentleness. I looked for her to rate me sharply, as I deserved, for my forgetfulness, but she was in another mood. "I can read it now with more composure and understanding than before," she went on.

She tore open the envelope as she spoke and drew forth a letter, unfolded it, and there dropped from it a little piece of parchment which I instantly picked up and extended to her. But she was so engrossed in the letter that she did not see my action and paid no attention to my outstretched hand.

CHAPTER IV
SHOWS HOW TWO PIECES OF PARCHMENT WERE FITTED TOGETHER

UNDER the circumstances, therefore, and without a thought that my action might be considered a possible violation of confidence, I looked at the parchment I held in my hand. It was evidently the half of a larger sheet which had been torn in two. The right half was in my possession. A glance showed me that it was a part of a rudely-drawn map, apparently of an island, although, lacking the other half, of that I could not be quite certain. Being a seafaring man, I was familiar with maps and charts of all sorts but I must admit that I had never seen a map that looked exactly like that one. It was lettered in characters which were very old and quaint, and some figures in the upper right-hand corner appeared to indicate a longitude. The outlines of the map and the letters and figures were all very dim and faded and a longer and closer inspection than I could give it then would be needed to show just what they were.

My lady's letter was a short one, for she looked up from it presently, her eyes filled with tears, the first I had seen there, and for that reason I was glad she could enjoy this relief. I suppose the fact that she was so alone and had no one else induced her to confide in me. At any rate, she extended the paper to me.

"Read it," she said. "'Tis my father's last word to me."

I took it from her and this is what I read:—

My Dear Lucy:

As an ancient King of France once said, everything is lost but honor, and that trembles in the balance. I have speculated, gambled, tempted fortune; first because I loved it and at last hoping to win for you. But everything has gone wrong. You are penniless, even your mother's fortune, of which she foolishly made me trustee, has followed my own. Master Ficklin may save something from the wreck. I hope so. I can do no more and perhaps, nay certainly, the best thing I can do for you is to leave you. May God help you since I cannot.

> Your shamed and unhappy father,
> GEOFFREY WILBERFORCE.

> Post Scriptum: The last thing that I possess is this scrap of parchment. It has been handed down from father to son for five generations. The tradition of it is lost, but there has always been attached to it a singular value. Perhaps some day the missing part may turn up. There used to be a little image with it, but that has disappeared, too. At any rate, of all that I once had, this alone is left. Should you marry and have children pass it to them, a foolish request, but I am moved to make it as my father made it to me.
>
> G. W.

I read it slowly. It was not a brave man's letter. I liked Sir Geoffrey less then than ever before. Some of the ancient awe and reverence I felt for the family went out of my heart then. Well, the man was dead, and there was no use dwelling on that any longer. I handed the letter back to Mistress Lucy without comment. As she took it I extended the parchment in the other hand.

"Here," said I, "is the enclosure to which your father refers. It seems to be a chart or map but in its torn condition it is of but little use."

She took it listlessly, but as her glance fell upon it her face brightened.

"Why!" she exclaimed, brushing aside her tears, "I, myself, have the other half and also the image."

I stared at her stupidly, not in the least taking in her meaning and she evidently resented my dullness.

"I have the other half of the parchment, the missing portion of the map, and the little idol, I tell you," she urged.

"You don't mean to say—" I began in amazement.

"Yes," she interrupted, "they came to me from my mother. When she died five years ago she gave them to me with much the same account as my father writes. I have never shown them to anyone, never mentioned the circumstances, even."

"Why not?" I asked.

"I scarcely know. The torn map was valueless. I attached no special importance to the hideous little image. But now, now—"

"It is a miracle," I said, "that the two pieces should have come together in your hands."

"I don't yet understand what it all means," she said, "but—"

"Meanwhile," said I, "may I respectfully suggest that you get the other piece and the idol or image and let me look at them? I know something about such matters."

"You!" she flashed out in one of those sudden changes of mood, sometimes so delightful and sometimes the reverse.

"I am a seafaring man, as you know, Mistress," said I humbly, "and I have seen many strange gods in different parts of the world. Also I am accustomed to study maps and charts. Perhaps this may contain information vital to your fortunes which I can decipher more easily than another."

She nodded and went rapidly out of the room. In a few moments she came back with another piece of parchment and a little stone figure, which I glanced at and laid aside for the moment, fixing my attention on the parchments. I placed them side by side and the torn and jagged edges fitted into each other perfectly. I had laid them on a table and bent over them in great excitement, excitement on my part caused by her proximity rather than by the faded, yellow sheepskin.

"It is an island!" she exclaimed.

"Yes," said I.

"Where is it?" she asked.

I pointed with my huge index finger to the figures in the upper left-hand corner and the upper right-hand corner marked respectively latitude and longitude.

"That will tell us exactly."

"And you can find it?"

"If it be there, where the figures say it is, I can, as easily as I can find the park gate yonder."

She looked at me with a certain amount of awe. Evidently the nice possibilities of the art of navigation had not been brought to her attention. I went up several degrees in her respect it seemed because I knew something she did not. Well, she was to find out that I knew many things that she did not—but I must not boast.

"Why, that is wonderful!" she exclaimed.

"Not at all. It is done by seamen every day."

"Have you ever been there?"

"No," said I, "I have crossed the South Seas several times but I have never chanced upon that island or in fact sailed anywhere near that latitude or longitude."

"But you know where it is?"

"Exactly, and if I had my great chart of the South Seas here, I could put my finger upon it and show it to you."

"What," she asked, pointing with her own dainty finger in her turn, "is that ring around the island?"

"That will be a coral reef, I take it. They usually are broken at some point so that ships can sail within, but here is a complete circle enclosing the island. There seems to be no entrance anywhere. 'Tis unusual and most strange."

"Perhaps the man that drew the map made a mistake."

"I think not. The map has been made by a seafaring man, that is plain."

"I see, and the island itself is a circle," she said, bending to inspect it more closely.

"Yes," said I, "and it is like no island that I have ever seen, for here be two great rings like a gigantic wall and a hill or something of the sort in the middle." I bent lower over it in my turn. My eyes are unusually keen and I saw words written on the outside of the island proper and between it and the coral reef. "See," said I, "the words 'ye stairs'!"

"Stairs!" exclaimed the girl in amazement, "did you ever see stairs on such an island?"

"No, I have not. But these may only be some natural means of ascent."

"It is most strange and meaningless," she said.

"Not so, my lady," I said, "these torn halves of the map have not been preserved through generations and handed down from father to son, or daughter, so carefully unless there be some meaning attached to them. What do you know about it? Forgive the presumption of my inquiry, but in this matter perhaps I can be of more service to you than I could be in anything else."

"You have been a faithful, devoted servitor, Master Hampdon," she said, "and I have no hesitation in telling you all I know. My mother and father were distantly related, that is they were descendants in the fifth generation from two brothers."

"Exactly," said I, "your father's note says this piece of parchment has been in possession of his family for five generations and evidently the other was in the possession of your mother's people for the same time."

"Why, that must be so," said the girl amazed, "indeed, I think you are very acute to have reasoned it out."

"I have but anticipated your own reflections, I am sure," said I. "Who was the father of these two brothers?"

She thought a moment.

"Sir Philip Wilberforce was his name. He was—"

"A sailor!" I exclaimed on a venture.

"You have guessed rightly; he voyaged in distant seas in Queen Elizabeth's time. It is reported that he was one of the first who went around the world after Sir Francis Drake showed all Englishmen the way."

"Exactly," I cried, "we are on the right track now. What further?"

"It is in my mind," she said, "that Geoffrey and Oliver, his sons, quarreled over his property after his death, and—"

"There you have it. They divided his fortune and tore the parchment apart, it being thought valuable for some reason, and each kept half," I returned confidently.

"That is the tradition as regards the fortune, and it may account for the parchment," she admitted in admiration of my conclusion, though indeed it was an easy one to draw.

"What next, madam?"

"The families drifted apart and gradually died out until Sir Geoffrey and my mother were alone left of their respective lines, and without knowing the relationship at the time they met and married, and I—" she faltered and put her hand over her face—"am the only one left of the family, of either branch."

"Now here," said I devoutly, for I fully believed what I said, "are the workings of Divine Providence. The parchment came from old Sir Philip, it was torn apart by his sons, and the pieces came not together until in you the ancient lines were united."

"Yes, but what does it mean?" she asked turning to the table again.

As she did so the sleeves of her dress caught the parchment and separated the two pieces. One of them fell to the floor face downward. I picked it up.

"Why, there is writing on it!" I exclaimed.

"So there is. I had forgotten that. It was unintelligible to me and, in fact, I put it in my jewel case and forgot about it."

"And the image?"

"It was so hideous and so repellent I thrust it into a drawer of my cabinet and forgot it too."

"Let's put the two pieces together and take them to the light and see if we cannot decipher it," said I. "Mistress Wilberforce," I continued, "I have a sailor's premonition that we are on the track of something that may greatly better your fortunes."

There was no table near the window but I spread the two pieces of parchment on my two broad hands, from which you can get an idea of how large they were. The writing was dim and faded with age. It seemed to have been done with some sharp pointed instrument which cut into the sheepskin, and where the ink which had been used had faded, the scratches still remained. This that follows is what I made out. I have reproduced exactly the old spelling and capitalization, and for your further illumination I have copied as best I could the map, or chart, upon the other side, so you can easily comprehend the story of our adventures upon it as I am now endeavoring to relate them. Of course my memory may be at fault in some particulars, but if so they are unimportant. As for the image, I can never forget its grinning, malign, evil hideousness, no, not to my dying day.

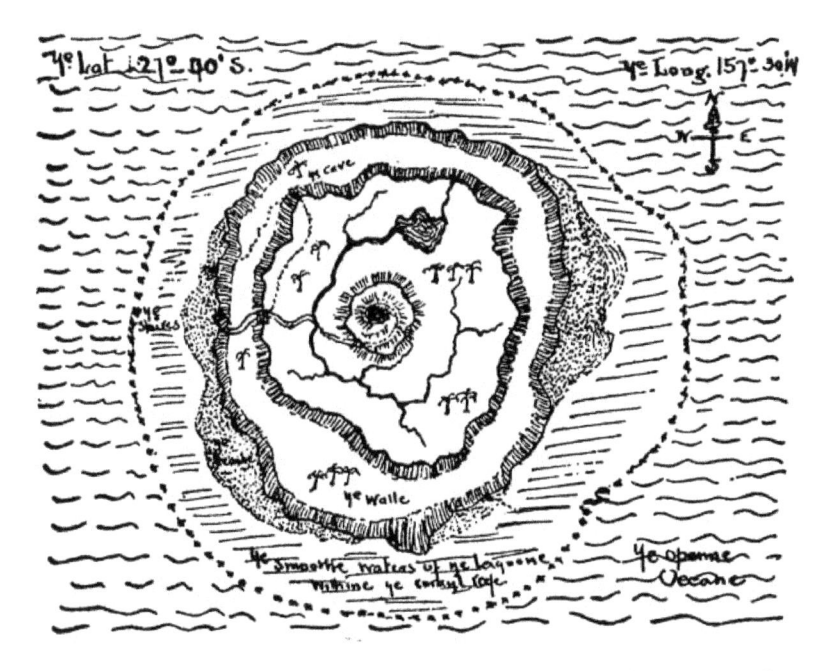

In ye yeare of oure Lorde 1595, I, Philip Wilberforce, Bt., of ye countie of Devon, being ye captaine of ye good shippe *Scourge of Malice*, didde take ye grate Spanish Galleon *Nuestra Senora de la Concepcion* after a bloudie encountre, wherein mine own shippe was sunke. Ye lading of ye galleon was worthe muche monaie, milliones of pounds esterling, I take yt. Withe manie jewelles and stones of price, pieces of eight and bullione, together with silkes and spicerie. Being blowne to ye southe and weste manie days in a grate tempeste, ye galleon was caste away on Ye

Islande of ye Staires. Wee landed ye tresor and hidde yt in ye walle. Alle my menne being in ye ende dead ye natives came over ye seas from ye other Islandes in their grate cannos and tooke me, being like a madde manne. Godde mercifullie preserving my life, I escaped frome themm and at last am comme safe intoe mine own sweet lande of Englande once more. Toe finde ye mouthe of ye tresor cave, take a bearing alonge ye southe of ye three Goddes on ye Altar of Skulles on ye middel hille of ye islande. Where ye line strykes ye bigge knicke in ye walle withe ye talle palmme tree bee three hoales. Climbe ye stones. Enter ye centre one. Yt. is there. Lette him that wille seek and finde. Here bee two of ye littel goddes I picked uppe and fetched awaye. Ye others are lyke onlie muche larger.

I spelt out the letters slowly, deciphering the quaint, faint writing with difficulty. Mistress Lucy drew near to me, bending over the parchment closely, following my efforts, indeed anticipating them with her quicker eye. Her presence was a distraction to me, yet I was so glad to have her near me that I wished the parchment letter as long as this story I am writing bids fair to be. Well, we finished it at last.

Then I turned to the table in the center of the room where I had left the image. I stooped over it, picked it up and brought it to the light. It was a head, with the neck and the top of the shoulders showing, mounted on a pedestal roughly cut in imitation masonry. It was made of some hard pinkish stone like granite. There was no skill or nicety in its carving; it was rough and rude, inexpressibly so, and the marks of the chisel, or whatever the tool with which it had been carved, were quite apparent here and there; and yet years of exposure to wind and weather had smoothed it off in part. The evil face was long and the dog teeth fell over the protruding lip in a peculiarly brutal and ferocious way. There was sort of a crown on the head, the eyes were sightless, and the whole expression was revolting and beastly.

What kind of people made and what kind of people worshiped such a god I wondered. I was not surprised that my little mistress had hid it away, nor that the one that came down through Sir Geoffrey's line had been lost. If I had possessed it, I would have destroyed it long since. It fairly radiated evil, and the contrast between my lady's face, all sweetness, purity, and light and this hideous image was the more marked. She has since confessed that she drew the same contrast between it and what she was pleased to call my brave and honest countenance! But of that more anon. We stared from the image to the parchment and then looked wonderingly at each other.

There was much in the letter, of course, that we could not possibly understand. We could only comprehend it fully if we were lucky enough to stand beneath "ye Stone Goddes," of which I held a sample in my hand, on the island itself. Still the general purport was sufficiently clear. Sir Philip Wilberforce had evidently concealed a very considerable treasure there. If we could find it our fortunes would be made, or hers rather, for I swear I never thought of myself at all.

"Think you," my little mistress began at last, her pale face flushing for the first time, her bosom heaving quickly, "that the treasure may still be there watched over by those awful gods?"

She glanced at the image I still held in my hand as she spoke.

"Who can tell?" I answered. "I am probably as familiar with the South Seas and their islands as any sailor; which is not saying a very great deal, for there are thousands of islands in those unknown seas which have never been visited by man, by white men, that is, or by any race which preserves records. I have never heard even a rumor of the Island of the Stairs, yet it would seem to be sufficiently different from all other islands to have been published abroad if it had been discovered. Its latitude and longitude place it in unfrequented seas among others peopled by races of savage cannibals. I think it not at all unlikely that it may have remained unvisited by any who would appreciate the value of the treasure since Sir Philip's day."

"But would such treasure last so long?"

"Stored in a cave, gold and silver and jewels would last forever. Everything else would have rotted away probably."

"It says to the value of millions of pounds, you notice," she repeated thoughtfully, pointing to the parchment again.

"Aye," I answered, "there is nothing unusual or unbelievable in that; the cargoes of those old Spanish galleons ran up into the millions often, I have read."

"How could we get there?" she asked.

"If you had a ship," said I, "well commanded and found and manned you could reach the spot without difficulty."

"How much would it cost?"

Well, I quickly and roughly estimated in my mind the necessary outlay. Such a vessel as she would require might be bought for perhaps twenty-five hundred or three thousand pounds; provisioning, outfitting, together with the pay of the officers and the crew, would require perhaps from fifteen hundred to two thousand five hundred pounds more, or a total of between five and six thousand pounds. And she had but two!

I was about to tell her the prohibitive truth when the solution of the problem suddenly came to me. In one way or another I had been a fortunate voyager and I had saved up or earned by trading and one or two adventures in which I had taken part, something over four thousand pounds, which was safely lodged to my credit in a London bank. Her fortune was two thousand pounds. Alone she could do nothing, together we could accomplish it. I had no right to put the suggestion in her mind, but I did it.

"I should think," I said slowly, "that two thousand pounds would be ample to cover everything."

"Ah," she said triumphantly, "exactly the sum that Master Ficklin said was left of my mother's fortune."

"Yes," said I, and then I added in duty bound, "but you surely would not be so foolish, Mistress Wilberforce, as to risk your all in this wild goose chase?"

"If you were in my position, Master Hampdon, what would you do?" she asked pointedly.

"I am a man," I answered, "accustomed to shift for myself. I might take a risk which I would not advise you to essay."

"I must shift for myself, too," she said, her eyes sparkling. The Goddess Fortune which had ruined her father was evidently jogging her elbow. "Indeed, I shall take the chance," she persisted. "I am resolved upon it."

"But you could easily live on two thousand pounds for a long while," I urged, against my wish, for I was keen to go treasure hunting with her for a shipmate.

"Not such life as I crave. If I cannot have enough for my desires I would be no worse off had I nothing."

"But it is a long chance," I persisted, "upon which to risk your all."

"Master Hampdon," she said solemnly, "the fact of the separation of those two pieces of parchment for a century and a half, and the fact that they come together in me, one half received from each of the dead who in neither case knew of the existence of the other half, the fact that I am Sir Philip Wilberforce's last descendant through both the original heirs—see you not something providential in all this?"

"A strange coincidence," I admitted.

"More than that," she protested.

Well, I was arguing against my wishes and from a sense of duty, so I at last gave way. After all, the treasure might be there. If so, it was hers and it would be a shame not to get it. The pulse of adventure leaped in my veins.

"So be it," I said.

"Will you help me to make my arrangements, you are accustomed to the sea, and—"

"I will do more than that," said I, "with your gracious permission I will go with you."

"To the island?"

"To the end of the world," I replied, whereat she stared at me a moment, then looked away.

She extended her hand to me and I tried to kiss it like a gentleman. I made, no doubt, a blundering effort, but at least it was that of an honest man.

"I must go and get ready to go to Master Ficklin's in the town," she said softly. "You know the house."

I nodded.

"Come to me there tomorrow and we will talk further about the project."

"Can I be of any other service?"

"Not now," she answered, "you have been of great service already. I shall not forget it."

And so I turned and walked out of the hall, leaving her standing there for the last time, at least so we thought, the last little descendant of a brave race. But you never can tell what the future will bring forth. I little dreamed that she and I were to stand there again some day under quite different circumstances. It is a good thing for me that I did not dream that dream then. It would have turned my head if I had.

CHAPTER V
WHEREIN THE DUKE IS MARKED IN FAREWELL

WHEN we broached the subject of our treasure hunting expedition to Master Ficklin the next day at his house, he would not hear of it. He examined the parchment with interest, but pooh-poohed the tale because, forsooth, it had no legal standing and was couched in the language of the sea rather than in the dry verbiage of the law. He pointed out that he had only succeeded in saving this last two thousand pounds of my lady's fortune because he had skillfully concealed its existence from Sir Geoffrey, foreseeing that all that he could come at would be recklessly flung away in the baronet's mad battle with fortune. He felt, he admitted to us, some compunctions of conscience about having hidden this little remainder from his friend and patron, and then he pleaded artfully that as he had gone against his sense of right for the sake of preserving this money, his wishes as to the spending of it ought to be respected, especially when they concerned so intimately the welfare of my lady; for, he asked pertinently, what would happen to her when all was gone and she had found no treasure, the very existence of which he affected to disbelieve?

A very hard-headed, practical person was Master Ficklin. He was not cut out for an adventurer, that was patent. Still his statements and propositions were entitled to the highest consideration. His arguments, indeed, appealed to my better judgment and I seconded them to the best of my ability in spite of my own desires. I was born with a roving spirit, and in my own blood ran something of the gambling strain, and the longer I dwelt upon possible treasure the more alluring grew the prospect of searching for it, and the more certain I became that it was there. It is so easy to persuade ourselves of what we wish.

Besides, even if there were no treasure, I luxuriated in spirit at the thought of the long months' intimate companionship at sea with my Little Mistress. It is true she already honored me with her friendship, but in no other way could I hope to enjoy much of her society in the future. She was too young and too beautiful for obscurity. Sooner or later true men would love her, the gay world would seek her out, she would enter upon her proper station again, and then where would I be? Selfish! Aye, but I am frankly telling the truth in these rambling recollections, even to my own discredit, though my lady will not have it so.

But I had stern ideas of duty, too, and Master Ficklin's good sense ever appealed to me. Yet when did mere good sense serve to persuade a woman against her wish? My lady would fain challenge fortune on her own account. She was of age and what she had left was absolutely in her control, but had she been but sixteen I make no doubt she would have had her way. She has ever had that way and ever will have it, so far as I am concerned. Worthy Master Ficklin has gone to his well-earned rest these many years as I write, but I am quite warranted, I am sure, in saying the same thing for him.

Well, the end of it was she made over her two thousand pounds to me without requiring me to give any bond, which Master Ficklin would fain have insisted upon. This would have been embarrassing indeed for me for my bond would have been my own capital which I was going to embark in the enterprise in secret. I had saved up that money with no one knows what foolish dreams. I now realized these dreams possibly would come to nought. Well, what difference? I had no one dependent upon me, brother or sister I had never been blessed with, and father and mother were both dead long since. I was alone in the world. What need had I for the money?

I could always get a berth on a good ship as mate, or perhaps as master, for which I was fully qualified; and I could always earn enough for my needs and to spare. Let her have it whose need was great and whose desire was greater.

I might have bargained for a share of the treasure did we find any, but I scorned to do it. I would fain give all and expect nothing. There was a certain salve to my pride in becoming a benefactor to the woman I—But I must not anticipate in my story, trouble came soon enough, as you shall see.

At any rate, not being in too great a hurry, although I was constantly urged to action by my lady, who could scarce possess her soul in patience before she began her treasure hunting once she was resolved upon it, I looked about a good deal in order to get just what

I wanted. Finally from a merchant of Plymouth I purchased a stout little ship of three hundred and fifty tons burden called *The Rose of Devon*, which had been engaged in the West Indian and the American colonial trade. The name caught my fancy, too, for was not my Little Mistress the Rose of Devon herself? You that read may laugh at me for my posying thought if you will; I care not, for it is true.

It was my first design to have gone as master of her myself and my lady would fain have had it so, but after reflection I decided it were better to have a much older man than I to command so long as she went as passenger, so I engaged a worthy seaman, one Samuel Matthews, old enough to be my father, with whom I had often sailed, in fact the man under whom I made my first cruise. I did engage myself as mate, however, and I even tried to induce Master Ficklin and his sister to go with us, whereat that worthy couple held up their hands in horror, preferring the one his musty parchments and suits at law, and the other her well ordered house and spacious garden. I was not sorry for their decision. I wanted to be alone on that ship with Mistress Wilberforce, with what vague idea or aspiration I dared not admit even to myself.

It seemed proper, in venturing among islands filled according to common report with savage peoples, to make ready for fighting; therefore, after consulting with Captain Matthews, whom I fully acquainted with the entire project in all its details, I shipped a crew of thirty men and I provided in the equipment plenty of muskets, pistols, and cutlasses with the necessary powder and ball and, in addition, a small brass cannon which I mounted on the forecastle. Nor did our cargo lack means for friendly trading and barter among the natives should such be found practicable.

Naturally, the unusualness of these preparations attracted some little attention and although Captain Matthews and I kept the destination of the ship and the purpose of the cruise strictly private, we were overwhelmed with applications from adventurous men who desired to make the voyage, surmising that it was after treasure of some sort and that it would be vastly different from the monotony of an ordinary merchant trading cruise. Clearance papers were got out for

The Island of the Stairs

the South Seas, which added the touch of romance that those waters always have, for an appeal.

Being so engaged with these larger matters, perforce I left the work of signing on a crew to Captain Matthews. He had as boatswain a veteran seaman named Pimball in whom he placed great confidence. He was a villainous looking man with a white scar running from his left eye across his cheek, caused by a cut he had received in some fight, and the line of white showing against the bronzed, weather-beaten cheek he sported, did not improve his appearance. But that he was a prime seaman was evident. Captain Matthews reposed much trust in him, somewhat to my surprise, for I was not prepossessed by his appearance, but the contrary. In answer to my objections he pointed out that many a man's looks belied his character, and although Pimball was certainly ugly, he was undoubtedly able. He had cruised several voyages with Captain Matthews and had always shown himself both experienced and dependable, so I let it go and he and Pimball selected the rest of the crew. It had been better for us in the end if I had got rid of the man as I wished. Or would it? Well, it would certainly have been better for Master Pimball and his friends.

To anticipate, when we boarded the ship I liked the crew not much better than the boatswain. I will say this for them, however, that a smarter, quicker set of seamen never hauled on brace or lay out on yardarm. It was not their skill or strength or courage that I misliked, no man could fault that, but they were not the sort of men I would have sought for a ship of my own; and the presence of my lady and her maid, a worthy woman, a long time servant at the castle, who had elected to follow her fortunes, perhaps made me unduly timorous; yet I was not unusually or extremely apprehensive. I had a sublime confidence in my own ability to deal with any man or any group of men. I had no doubt that Captain Matthews and I would be able to master them and bend their wills to ours at the cost of a few hard words backed by a ready rope's end or a well-used marlinspike or belaying pin.

I did not stint the outfitting of the ship, and when I finished, having left nothing out of her manifest that either mine own or Captain Matthew's experience or imagination could suggest, including everything conceivable for the comfort of my lady, there remained of our joint funds enough to pay the wages of the officers and of the men out and back and no more. That is allowing a year for the round voyage. The lines of *The Rose of Devon* were unusually good; she had a reputation for being a speedy vessel, and that was more time than enough. It was my purpose to go on around the world with her rather than retrace our course about Cape Horn after we reached the island, if we ever reached it. So we staked everything we had on the future. If my lady had possessed the least knowledge of the value of ships, she would have seen how little way her two thousand pounds had gone, but she was as guileless as any other woman on that subject, and Master Ficklin was not much better. I lied to them both, although with a somewhat uneasy conscience. Yet it was for her sake. My family had followed hers for I know not how many centuries. They had spent themselves for hers. I was only keeping up the traditions in placing all that I had at her service.

But one thing which happened before we embarked occurs to me as worthy to be chronicled. When all was ready and everything aboard, I went back to Master Ficklin's in Tavistock, which was an easy day's journey from Plymouth Sound, where *The Rose of Devon* lay, to fetch my lady and her maid. Master Ficklin's house was a somewhat large one for an attorney and was surrounded by a walled garden, perhaps two acres in extent, which ran from the back of the house to a little brook which bounded the village. There were a number of fine old trees in it and much shrubbery and it was a pleasant place in which Mistress Wilberforce and I had spent some, to me, very delightful hours in perfecting the plans for our great undertaking.

Master Ficklin was at his office, although it was yet early in the morning when I called, intending to fetch my lady to Plymouth by coach, a special coach which I had engaged for her particular use, by the way. His sister said that Mistress Wilberforce was in the garden and that she had company. She offered to show me to her presence, but I said I knew the way and could go myself. I did not like the word company over much. Her fine friends had more or less forgot her. One or two of the old families which had been associated with hers had offered her such hospitality and such comfort as they had, until she could decide otherwise; some of the women had called upon her, one or two men had sought her out, but she was a proud

The Island of the Stairs

little woman, as you can divine, and would have none of them. She had dropped out of their lives and latterly no one had disturbed her, therefore I was perturbed at the tidings.

I passed though the hall, out of the back door and into the garden. The path to the brook wound and twisted so that you could not see the stream for the trees and shrubs. I stood a moment, hesitating, wondering whether after all I had the right or the privilege to break in upon such company as she might be entertaining, when a scream which came faintly from the end of the garden, decided me.

I broke into a run and in a few moments came upon my lady struggling in the arms of a man. What man, do you ask? None other than his grace, the Duke of Arcester! He had his arms around her and although he was no great figure of a man, he was much stronger than the slight girl he was grappling so roughly. He held her tightly by the waist with one arm and with the other was trying to turn her head so that he could kiss her fairly on her lips.

I was upon them before either realized my arrival. In my fury I grasped the duke by the collar of his coat with my left hand and with my right I ruthlessly tore him away from my lady.

"Thank God, you have come!" she cried, reeling and staggering, her face flushed, her hair disheveled, her dress in disarray.

I heard that much and then the duke was upon me. Gritting his teeth and swearing frightful oaths, he got to his feet—I had thrown him prone—dragged out his sword and rushed at me.

"You dog!" he cried, "you have balked me before and you interfere now. I have had enough of you, and the world has."

He did not intend to give me any chance to defend myself apparently. My little mistress screamed. I heard her call my name and I suppose she thought I was done for, but sailors are proverbially quick-witted, footed, and handed, and I was not the least alert of seamen for all my size. I was wearing a hanger, a much heavier and more unwieldly weapon than the duke's dress sword, but its weight was a matter of no moment to an arm like mine. I sprang aside as he lunged furiously at me, drew it, and the next moment our blades clashed in earnest. For myself, I rejoiced in the opportunity. Some men of humble birth might have been disturbed at the thought of crossing swords with a great noble, but nothing of that occurred to me. I wanted to show my lady, I confess, that even with gentlemen's weapons I was this man's master. And so I fell to it eagerly.

Now I am a good fighter and no mean fencer. I can cross blades with anyone on earth. I did not know all the niceties and refinements of the game. I lacked grace perhaps—but when it came to attack and defense, there were few men who could beat me—certainly the duke was not one of them. My swift play must have looked to the duke as if I were surrounded by a wall of steel. Therefore, he realized at once that his only chance lay in the energy and rapidity of his fence. He was as passionately incensed as I, if from a different cause. Lunge succeeded lunge with lightning-like speed. I will admit that I was hard put to it for a time. The play of light on his blade fairly dazzled me. It was with the greatest difficulty that I parried. But my lord was not built for the long continuance of such violent exercise. Sweat ran into his eyes, his thrusts grew less swift, less sure, if not less vicious in their intent. I could feel his growing weakness with my blade. After a few moments I saw that I had him. It was now my turn to attack. Something of the berserk madness of my Saxon ancestors suddenly filled my veins. I beat down his defense by a series of terrific blows and finally shivered his sword. He stood before me panting, weaponless, yet to give him his due, more or less undaunted. I raised my own blade.

"Would you strike a defenseless man, cur?" he cried haughtily, still not blenching.

"You had no scruple in attacking a defenseless woman," I replied. "Nay," I thundered as he made a sudden movement, "stand where you are. What I shall do to you depends upon what I hear. If you move I swear to you that I will beat you down like the villain that you are."

I was amazed afterward at my temerity in thus addressing a duke, but you will understand my feelings. Without taking my eyes off of him, I next addressed myself to my lady, who had shrunk aside and watched us breathlessly.

The Island of the Stairs

"Will you tell me now, Mistress Lucy," said I softly, "what this man proposed or said? I can see what he did, but what were his meaning and intent?"

"He—he—wanted—me to go with him," faltered my lady.

"He renewed his offer of marriage?" I asked with a sudden sinking of heart.

I had a good deal of reverence for the nobility except in the heat of battle, and even as bad a man as Arcester was nevertheless a duke and a great personage. That should mean something to a woman. Perhaps my lady might wish to marry him after all!

"No," whispered the girl, and at her answer my blood burned for her.

"My God!" I cried, "did you dare to—"

"Why should I marry a penniless baggage?" he sneered. It was a reckless thing to do, seeing his helpless position. "She would not go with me, she refused even to take my hand, the little fool, so I seized her. Was it because she preferred you, yokel?" he added.

"For whatever reason she refused the proffered honor, she has had a lucky escape."

"Perhaps so, clodhopper, for I should have discarded and forgot her when her prettiness had faded, but you—"

"I shall ensure that you will remember all the days of your life what you tried to do; the insult that you put upon this lady," I said quietly, although I was blazing inside.

"Would you kill me?" he cried, and I believe I detected a note of alarm in his voice for the first time, as I stepped nearer to him.

"No," said I, "that would be too quick and easy an end to your punishment. I will put my mark upon you, her brand as a blackguard. Everybody who sees you will ask you about it and you can explain it as you will. Two persons at least will know what the mark signifies, my lady and myself."

He stared at me absolutely uncomprehending, but before he could make a move I caught him around the breast, pinioned both his arms to his side with one arm and then I deliberately shortened my sword, holding it by the blade, and cut two long, deeply scored, rough gashes crosswise in his right cheek. He struggled and shrieked horribly as I did so and my lady screamed as well, but I held him close until I finished. He was a handsome man, but those two scars, roughly crisscrossed, would never be eradicated, for I had cut deep with deliberate purpose.

"Now," said I to my little mistress, "before I release him one more question. Did he—did he kiss you?"

"No," answered Mistress Wilberforce faintly.

"Good," I continued grimly, "had he done so I had marked the other cheek."

After that assurance of hers I released him and he staggered back, trembling and shaking, spitting blood, his cheek bleeding, a horrible looking object.

"That will be a lesson to your grace," said I grimly, "not to insult an honest woman. I have no doubt there are many who would rejoice to see you now and to know why I have put my mark upon you."

"I will have the law on you. I will have your life," he sputtered out.

"You can have anything you want," said I recklessly. "I am your master with the sword, and your master with everything else. Now go."

He turned and staggered away and that was the last I saw of him. I heard later that he had had the devil's own time explaining those marks. He proclaimed that they had been inflicted by a madman, which was nearly the truth, but in some way the story leaked out and I should judge that my vengeance for the insult to my lady was as adequate as anything could be. He never lived down the tale, and I take it he was glad when he received a mortal wound in a duel from the hand of some other avenger of a woman's wrong some years later.

"Master Hampdon," whispered Mistress Lucy, in an awe-struck voice, as we went together through the garden, while I wiped my sword with leaves, "why did you do that? 'Twas horrible."

"Why, mistress," said I, striving to speak formally, "when I saw you in his arms I could have killed him."

"But to mark him thus forever—" she began.

"Enough," said I, with one of those flashes of imperiousness which always amazed me afterward and which really seemed to affect her strangely, "he only got his deserts."

"But he will take his revenge on you," she persisted.

"Let him try," said I indifferently. "But I am come to take you to the ship. We must get there tonight to sail with the beginning of the ebb tomorrow morning."

"I am ready," she said, putting her hand upon my arm with unwonted humility.

We went into the house and from there to the coach with her maid and her baggage, after making her farewells to her kind host and hostess. In the evening we got aboard the ship where I saw her safely bestowed in the comfortable cabin I had arranged for her and for her woman. When day broke and she came on deck, we were under way for the Island of the Stairs. The great adventure had begun.

BOOK II

ABOARD SHIP IN THE SOUTH SEAS

The Murderous Mutineers and the Woman

CHAPTER VI
IN WHICH I AM PUNISHED FOR MY PRESUMPTION

I PASS over the events of the next six months without comment, but not because they were uninteresting. Oh, no. One could not sail from Plymouth, England, to the South Seas, touching at Madeira, the Canaries, Rio and Buenos Ayres and rounding the mighty and fearsome Cape Horn, without seeing many things of interest and participating in scenes as dangerous as they were exciting. But I am not writing a book of travels, though perchance I may some day endeavor to set forth for your delectation some of my far voyagings in unknown seas. Suffice it to say that we passed safely from the much traversed Atlantic to the lonely Pacific, and were drawing near to the island we sought according to the calculations of good Captain Matthews and myself, when something happened.

I had brought it on myself, I realized, but that made it no more bearable. Indeed, I was mad, mad all through; outraged in dignity, humiliated in self-respect, and were it not foolish to speak so of a man of my years and standing, I should say I was broken in heart. I suppose that I should feel the wound to my affections more than that to my pride later, but at that present moment feelings of indignation predominated. I had been a fool, of course, and I should have expected nothing else; equally, of course, perhaps I should even have anticipated this, and probably if I had been in my right senses on that day I would have known it. But then you see, I was not in my right senses, and that was the secret of my disgrace. And that it all happened after half a year of the friendliest, most pleasant intercourse between a man and a maid only intensified the bitterness of the situation.

My little mistress had been so kind to me that I had dwelt in a fool's paradise. I awoke to realize that she had not forgot the difference between our stations. She had been born in the castle, I in the gardener's lodge; she was of the great house, I was of the cottage. I had forgot it in these long months at sea — by heaven, the sight of her was enough to make a man forget anything if he loved her as I! There, the secret is out, though I make no doubt you guessed it long before — but it seems she had not. There was no mirror in the cabin, but I could well guess that the sight of me was not sufficiently prepossessing to make any woman forget our respective merits and stations.

In birth, in breeding, in education, in everything, she stood immeasurably removed from me; so far removed that association on any terms scarcely seemed possible. Yet she had been so kind. I was her only confidant or companion in the ship. I had forgot all that lay between, or else, remembering, I had yet endeavored to leap the gap. I had fondly hoped that the one thing in me that was truly great, my passion for her, would land me safely by her side. I did not see how she could fail to comprehend it, though I did try to disguise it.

Well, that love of mine — it had not brought her nearer. On the contrary it had put me under lock and key! And here I was, shut up like a criminal in my own cabin in her ship, or mine for that matter. Come to think of it, that moment I believe love had completely disappeared. I could recall — and can to this day — the fierce, burning rush of color to her cheek where I had kissed it; the fire of rage and surprise mingled which sparkled in her eyes. The Duke of Arcester I had marked for life for less than this, I recalled in shame.

I hardly recollected the fierce blow of her hand upon my face. That was nothing. I had laughed at it as she had recoiled from me when I had released her — actually laughed! I was not laughing at her, God knows, but at her impotence physically compared to my strength. She was a small slender little body, I could have carried her easily with my one hand — and I have often done so since — yet she struck hard when she did strike.

As I recalled it, I suppose that laugh was my undoing. Perhaps she thought I laughed at her. Well, what mattered it? Whatever the cause, I was undone. All the patient devotion of years, all the restraint of the long voyage had come to naught.

There had been plenty of bright starlight on deck. She had stepped out from the dark shadow of the spencer and I had followed hard on her heels. The first night watch had not yet been called and the men idle about the decks, waiting the boatswain's shrill whistle, had noted it all. I can see their sneering, laughing faces even now. God! I could bear anything from her but nothing from them, and but for the sorry figure I must have cut in a low brawl with the ruffians, I would have leaped upon them and fought them until they killed me.

As it was, I drew myself up and waited while she sent for good old Captain Matthews and, vouchsafing no explanations, imperiously bade him stow me below as a prisoner in my cabin. He didn't relish the job but went about it forthwith. Indeed, I did not wait for further orders after her look and glance. I stalked below as haughtily as you please. It was her ship, as she had said and as she certainly believed, and had it not been, who could deny her anything? Not I, forsooth. I could steal a kiss but not balk her will.

So here I was, the mate of *The Rose of Devon*—and but for my own renunciation I had been her captain—engaged in this wild goose chase, this foolish search for treasure, for so it seemed to me then, locked up below like any mutinous dog at the behest of a woman that I could have broke between my thumb and finger. And after all I had done and sacrificed for her, too.

The hot blood came into my cheeks again. I remember I raised my arm and shook it toward the door and then let it fall. What was the use? I was her prisoner. I loved her, fool that I was. I thought then and I think now I had rather be her prisoner than be free and away from her, than be free and know her not. No lovesick boy could have been more foolish than I about her—and, in your ear, I am so yet.

Come to think of it, I had always loved her, ever since those days when I, the gardener's boy, had been her faithful and devoted slave. And through the long years when I had been far voyaging in distant seas I had kept her memory fresh and sweet and true. I had been in many rough places, I had seen life from the seamy side, the common lot of a sailor of my day had been mine. I was not what you would call a religious man; no, not nearly religious enough, but the thought of her and my mother had kept me a clean man. In that respect, at least, I was worthy of her; doubtless, I dare say, more worthy of her than Arcester and Luftdon and all the young gallants who had paid court to her before her father lost his all and had blown out his brains, leaving her but the parchment and enough gear with my aid to charter and equip the ship.

Such as it was, my heart was hers, and my life had always been. As often as I could I had come back to the old cottage where I was born and for old time's sake she had been kind to me. I had craved even her condescension, although it made me mad to see her surrounded by the other men and women, so that I would fling myself away and take the first ship that offered to the farthest port. Yet, I always came back—to her.

And I had been so glad that I was there when Sir Geoffrey had killed himself and that I had bought the ship and fitted it out and had been able to do so much for her. As I said, she would fain have given me command of the saucy little *Rose of Devon* had I willed it—and sometimes, now for instance, I cursed myself that I had not taken it rather than insisted that she should have an older man, not a better seaman, than I. There are no better seamen in narrow seas or broad than I, if I do say it myself, who should not.

I had worked my way up through the forecastle to the quarter-deck. I had a natural gift for figures. I could take a sight and work out a position as well as any book-taught navigator, and I had been a great reader, too. My private cabin was crowded with books. A goodly portion of my earnings was ever spent that way. I had wit enough to choose good books, too, and perseverance enough to study them well. And they stared at me then from shelves built in the bulkhead. What fond dreams I had indulged in while I had pored over them, turning their thin pages with my tarred, blunt fingers! I walked over to them that night and struck them with my fist in impotent rage. What was the use of it? The stain of tar was on me forever in her eyes.

And yet I knew more than she. Oh, much more about everything but the usages of good society, and I had at least learned something of good manners in her company since her father's death. Many a time

The Island of the Stairs

I have caught her tripping as to facts of knowledge, not daring, not even caring to tell her; or, perhaps I had better say, not wishful to humiliate her by showing her that she was wrong, content to know that much myself, and hugging my poor little superiority to my heart. I knew more than she and more than most of the men with whom she associated. My shipmates used to laugh at me for being a book delver, a worm, they were wont to call me. Well, they didn't laugh very long. There was nothing physical for which I need stand aside for any man. I was over six feet high and built in proportion. I could unaided, and alone, hold the wheel of the best ship in the fiercest storm. I had matched myself against man and against storm, not once but many times, and neither the one nor the other had ever made me back down.

Now I was a prisoner. I said I didn't feel that blow on the cheek, but as I thought on it, it fairly seared me. I hated her, I hoped that—no, I might as well be honest with myself—I didn't care how she treated me, how disdainful were her words, how unjustly she punished me, I loved her. I couldn't help it, I didn't want to help it. I would fain kiss the deck planks she hallowed with her footsteps.

There was another side to my confinement and I presently took thought on that. I swear that I was not thinking of myself but of her. I was ever thinking of her. I could see dangers that beset her as perhaps no one else could, and my confinement added to her peril. She didn't realize that; nobody aft on the ship realized it. I did not see any present way to make her understand the situation. I had not cared to alarm her before, and any attempt on my part to set it forth now would be looked upon as a personal plea, and yet there was a peril, imminent, menacing, about to break, I feared.

You see, the fact that we were treasure hunting had got about. Who told it I could not discover, but the unusualness of our proceedings, the arming of a peaceful merchant ship, the indefiniteness of the articles, the clearing from Plymouth for the South Seas, the absence of any great amount of cargo, and the high wages promised had aroused suspicions. I had not thought much about the crew, except of Pimball. We had shipped a lot of smart seamen; about the average in quality and above the average in smartness, I decided as the days had passed with nothing happening; but times were good and ships were plenty, and we had sailed rather late in the season, and Pimball had signed many I could wish had been left ashore.

Her presence on the ship, too, was a mystery. Alone in the little *Rose of Devon* with thirty men! By evil mishap the maid she had brought with her had died after a brief illness two weeks out. Captain Matthews and I were for turning back, but she said no, she would go on. We had lost too much time already and her all was embarked. We were now plowing the blue waters of the Pacific and I, mate of the ship, and the only other officer to be trusted, locked up! Pimball, the boatswain, seemed to me to be the least trustworthy of the lot. I had not got over my initial dislike for him at all!

We were nearing the latitude and longitude of the island. Suppose the men rose in mutiny! I ground my teeth in rage at the thought. The men liked me well enough, and I had been particular to keep them in good humor, passing over many a thing for her sake that I would have followed with a blow had she not been there. Captain Matthews had complained once or twice of my laxity, but I knew things that he didn't, and I had done what I deemed best for her. I pledge you my word that I didn't care a farthing for the treasure. I had never given it much thought. I grew to believe in it less and less as we got further from home, and if I had been stronger for my duty and weaker in my love I would have dissuaded her from the voyage, following Master Ficklin's lead.

Now that she was poor and alone, neglected and forgotten, I had enjoyed a foolish dream that I could be a companion to her—a life shipmate!—for the captain was a rough, plain old sailor. What a fool I was! and yet it had worked in some way as I had intended. We had been thrown into closer intimacy by the loneliness of her position, and by my faithful and, until that night, most unobtrusive, self-effacing devotion. I was thinking too much of her to give my attention to any other kind of treasure anyway, and I'd rather have had her than all the golden argosies that plowed the seas.

I supposed it never entered her head that I could presume to love her, consequently she was less careful than she had been otherwise, and that very night when I had poured out my declaration to her, she had found no words with which to meet it. I thought her motionless silence was consent. I see now that it was petrified

The Island of the Stairs

amazement. I seized her in my arms, like the brute she must have thought me, lifted her up and kissed her fair on the lips and then on her averted cheek. Arcester, the blackguard, could have done no worse. I will never forget how she stigmatized me, brute, coward, lowborn. I don't believe she had railed at that scoundrel duke so fiercely. Well, I didn't care what she called me. Her safety, her life, her honor demanded that I be released. That was the paramount concern.

I listened—I thought I heard a footfall in the outer cabin. Could she be there? I suppose that I had been locked up for perhaps an hour, aye, on the instant the bell forward struck three. We kept man-o'-war customs at her fancy. The sound came to me faintly as I listened. Half past nine. She could not have gone to her berth yet. She must be there in the great cabin. I ventured to call.

Any man can imagine what it cost me to humble myself to ask her mercy. Stop, I ought to apologize. No gentleman—I do not mean the dandies that made love to her—but no real gentleman such as I, in spite of my low birth and rough breeding, hoped I might prove myself to be, would have taken advantage of her as I did. Yes, an apology was certainly owing from me. Even had it not been I should have been compelled to make it for her sake.

I am a man of fierce temper, as you have deemed and as you shall see, if you go with us further in this history, but I can control it on occasion, and I did it now. I shook the door of the cabin gently at first and then vigorously and called once and again. There was no answer. I beat upon it. I raised my voice. I scarcely thought I could be heard on deck. The wind was blowing, the sea was heavy and the ship was pitching wildly, the straining, the creaking, the groaning of the timbers would have prevented such a noise as I made from attracting attention unless someone were in the cabin.

But all in vain. No heed was paid to me and yet I could swear that somebody was there. I don't know how exactly, but I was conscious of her presence. Perhaps because I was so in love with her that I could always tell whether she was about. I can to this day. Many a time in after years she has stepped into the room where I have been sitting, without a sound, and has come to me and laid her hand on my shoulder, but I have had knowledge before she touched me that she was there.

It made me madder than before to go thus unheeded. I was on the point of giving over my endeavor, but the thought of that peril in which she stood, and the fact that I was removed from the deck and a prisoner, made me resolve on one more effort. She must be made to hear, and if to hear, to answer.

"Madam," I whispered softly, and then more loudly, "Madam!"

I did not venture to say any other name. I called again and yet a fourth time and then for the last time with the full power of my voice. I heard a movement outside and then a voice, beloved, blessed voice even when it rated me!

"Well, sir."

The words came to me through the partition. She was there then, as I had divined. She had been there all the time, trying me.

"I would fain have a word with you," I answered, putting everything else by and speaking most entreatingly and with a humility I did not altogether feel.

"I desire no speech with you," was her cold and measured answer.

I could hear her turn as if to move away. She had come very softly, but she went loudly as if to show me her intention.

"Think of my long and faithful service," I urged, "and of your gracious friendship for me, often expressed."

"You yourself forgot it tonight."

"For God's sake," I cried desperately as I heard her go, "just one word."

"An apology? Do you beg for forgiveness?"

"No—yes—anything," I finished in confusion.

"I will not listen. I wish to convince you of the enormity of what you have done, the grossness of your presumption. I will give you time for quiet reflection, sir."

"I am convinced already," I urged hurriedly.

The Island of the Stairs

"So easily," she mocked.

"Madam, if you love life and honor, I pray you hear me. It is not of myself I think but of you. You are in grave peril," returned I with the utmost seriousness.

"What peril?"

There was a note of alarm in her voice in spite of her effort to be indifferent. I seized upon its promise eagerly.

"The men of the ship, they are not what they should be. Captain Matthews is alone. Pimball is a villain. I trust no one but—"

"And is that the plea on which you seek your freedom?"

"That is the only plea."

"You did not discover this danger until I locked you up, did you?"

She laughed mockingly, but there was music in her voice for me, albeit her words were harsh and unjust.

"I tell you that it is not for myself I fear, but for you," I persisted.

"And was it for that you insulted me on the quarter-deck before the men and—"

"No," said I savagely. "By heavens, I did that for myself."

"Arcester could have done no worse," she said cuttingly.

"Curse Arcester!" I burst out, the mention of the man's name always inflaming me, "he would have made you his—"

"Silence!" cried the woman. "I will hear no more. It is a foolish plea, the men are devoted to me and—"

"For God's sake, Mistress Wilberforce," I cried, but this time she was gone.

I heard the door of her cabin shut violently. There was no help for it. Well, I must devise some way unaided. For I must get out for her sake. The cabin was lighted by an air port closed by a deadlight. I measured it, drew back the thick glass and examined the opening, although I knew it was a futile proposition. A slender boy might have slipped through but not a man such as I. My mighty thews and sinews and great bulk required a door and no small one, either.

The wind had increased, it was blowing hard outside and some spray came in through the port as the waves slapped the side of the ship. I closed and secured it; there was nothing to be gained there. I must seek some other way.

I was not weaponless. Nobody had thought to search my cabin, and a brace of pistols which I always kept loaded and ready for an emergency were locked securely in my chest. My hanger, none of your dandified French rapiers but a stout ship's cutlass, ground to a razor's edge, heavy enough to paralyze any arm but one muscled like mine, hung at the side of my berth. It was the same with which I had marked the duke.

The cabin door was a strong one. It was locked and barred without. I might have broken through it. I could have done so if I had had space enough in which to run and hurl myself against it. I might even have kicked it to pieces with my heavy seaman's boot. Certainly I could easily have blown the lock off with my pistol, but any of these endeavors would have aroused the ship.

To let the sleeping dogs lie when you have no means of controlling them should they awaken, I have ever found to be a good maxim. I had one other hope. If Captain Matthews should come to the cabin I would appeal to him. For the rest I determined not to sleep that night. Some strange foreboding possessed me, such a feeling a man has when his own hand is taken from the helm and no other is near by to grasp it, as if the uncontrolled ship must surely broach to and founder.

We were near the latitude and longitude of the island we were seeking, if indeed there were such an island as was thought to be, and I reasoned that the men would argue that now would be a good time for an outbreak, especially since I was removed. Would it come that night? Would it come at all? Was I mistaken in the men?

I have often wondered why women were made and, since they were made, why men should be such fools about them—yet I would by no means unmake them! Here I was helpless just because I had snatched a kiss from one. Although I had ever been a decent man as man goes, I had ventured as far as kisses with maidens here and there in this little world around which I had gone so many times, and none of them had ever taken it quite like that. To be sure, none of them was like her. And now that I am in the mood for confession, I might as well say that I fully rejoiced in that kiss. It had not been on the cheek first but full and fair on her lips, and I had held her tight and drunk my fill—no not that, of course; I could never do that, but still it had been a man's kiss on a maiden's lips fairly given, and—

Well, whatever happened, I had the memory of that kiss. She would never forgive me. Of course, there was absolutely no hope that she would return my suit even in her poverty. She was not for such as I, and if there was anything in this old buccaneer's parchment, if there was an island, if she did get the treasure, why the world would be at her feet again; and I, like the fool I was, was helping her get it, to bring that about. I was mad, aye, mad, with impotent helplessness that night.

I sat there in the dark, no light being vouchsafed to me and the lanterns in the outer cabin not having been lighted, for a long time. The wind rose and rose. The ship was pitching madly. My room was on the starboard side of the cabin and presently I heard all hands called to reef the topsails. Captain Matthews was alert and ready, of course. Presently he put the ship about and with some of the canvas off her she was steadier. There did not seem to be any especial danger in the weather and for that I was thankful.

I must have dozed. I was awakened by the last echoing of the bell forward. I didn't know what time it was because I didn't know whether I had heard it begin to strike, but I could count three couplets, which meant that it was eleven o'clock at least. I didn't know, of course, that it was eight bells, midnight, until after a shrill piping of his whistle the long-drawn-out voice of the boatswain came to me through the low bulkhead that separated the trunk cabin from the quarter-deck above and the 'tween decks below.

"A—a—all the port watch! Show a leg, lively, lads!"

I could hear the men of the watch below grumbling and cursing as they turned out. They had evidently been sent to their hammocks after the topsails had been reefed for a couple of hours in. I could also hear scraps of conversation as they struggled into their jackets and coats.

"Let's do it."

"Now?"

"Yes!"

"Shall we kill him?"

"This is the best time!"

"Aye, aye."

"The old man's alone!" and so on.

What I heard filled me with dismay. The purport was plain. I picked up the pistol and pointed it at the lock in the door. I had made up my mind, come what might, to blow off the lock and get free. Perhaps I could even yet prevent and overawe them. Before I could press the trigger, however, I heard a call on the deck above me, a shot, a rush of feet, a scuffle, oaths, curses, a cry for help, a groan, a fall!

CHAPTER VII
WHEREIN I BARGAIN FOR A WOMAN

WHAT dire misfortune had happened I could well guess. Captain Matthews had been attacked. He had promptly shot one of the mutineers, and thereafter the rest had killed him. My next impulse was to blow open the lock of the door as I had intended, and rush to avenge him, but wiser counsel prevailed and I did nothing. I am, I think, somewhat cool-headed in a crisis, and surely this was one. I could wait. A loaded pistol was better than an empty one, and to deal with me they would have to come to me for whatsoever purpose they might entertain, either to murder me or to release me. In either event I could do more than if I rushed headlong into the fray now. I could not help poor Captain Matthews. I was sure that whatever fell purpose they might entertain for my little mistress would be in abeyance until they had settled with me. I flattered myself that I was too important to be disregarded by the mutineers. Therefore, I carefully looked to my weapons, seeing to the priming and slipping an additional bullet in the barrel. After that I stood by the door, weapon in hand, grimly ready for the murderous mutineers.

I waited with every nerve strained to the utmost. I also listened most anxiously for the opening of the door of the after cabin which was her own, but she must have been in a sound sleep, indeed, for the door did not open. Evidently she had heard nothing, mercifully she had not been awakened. After all, if she had come into the main cabin I think I must have come out also, one way or another; but so long as she slept, and so long as I could force the door when I wished, I waited. It was not an easy task, but I judged it best.

Fortunately, I had not long to wait, for in less time by far than I have taken to tell it, the hatch was opened and a number of heavy-booted men clattered down the companionway. The cabin steward, of course, knew the arrangement of the after part of the ship and he brought them straight to my door. The key was in the lock outside and I could hear them turn it. I loosened my sword which I had slung by its belt around my waist, grasped my two pistols more firmly, set my back against the side of the ship and made ready for whatever came.

The door was pushed open abruptly and I saw the cabin was crowded with men. At least half the crew was assembled there, and it was a little cabin, *The Rose of Devon* being but a small ship. The rest, I guessed, were on watch. I could not see the boatswain, evidently he had the deck. The vessel could not be left unwatched on such a night as this and in such a sea, and he was the fittest man to take charge of her. The steward had lighted both the cabin lanterns, several of the men carried hand lanterns which they had brought from the forepeak. There was plenty of illumination to show their villainous faces.

They were surprised to find me so prepared and I gave them no time to recover.

"The first man," I hissed out, raising my firearms and leveling them at the group, "that tries to enter this berth without my permission gets a bullet through him!"

"We mean you no harm, sir," gruffly spoke out one who seemed to be a ringleader, a man rated as boatswain's mate, whose name was Glibby.

"What are you doing here," I asked, "in the cabin at this time of night?"

"Softly, softly, sir," replied Glibby, "we're here to arsk questions, not to answer 'em."

"What do you mean?" I cried.

"We're masters of the ship."

"Captain Matthews?"

"He'll cap'n no more ships on this or any other seas," answered Glibby with truculent emphasis.

Now it rose in my mind to shoot him then and there, murderous brute that he was—if I had been alone perhaps I would have done it without reckoning the consequences to myself, but I had another to think of. Unless craft stood me in good stead her case was hopeless.

And bad as Glibby was, Pimball was the chief villain. No, I decided, nothing much would be gained by killing the boatswain's mate when the boatswain lived. I trust no man will think me a traitor or craven for what I said next. The idea came to me on the instant and it seemed I could do no better than adopt it. God forgive me if it was wrong.

"Curse him!" I broke out with well simulated heat, "serves him right. He disrates me and locks me up here just for stealing a kiss from a maid, and—"

"Spoke like a man of spirit, Mister Hampdon," cried Glibby, greatly pleased evidently. "What did I tell ye, mates? He's with us."

"With you," said I, carelessly pointing my weapons downward but taking good care to keep them ready, "I am with you, all right. What do you propose? I am sick of the treatment I received, and—"

"We want that 'ere treasure for ourselves."

"And you shall have it, provided I get my share with the other men," I answered, scarcely startled by their words, for this I had expected.

"We'll share an' share alike in everything," answered Glibby. "Am I right, mates?"

"Right you are," came from the deep voices of the men.

"Aye," said Glibby, "ship an' treasure, an'—er—" with a frightful leer—"woman!"

God! How I longed to clutch him by his throat and choke him! My temper rose again, but this time, as before, I managed to keep it down though with immense difficulty, as you may suspect.

"Come out into the cabin, Mr. Hampdon," said Glibby with a certain complacent civility in his manner which he doubtless meant to be engaging, but for which I hated him the more if possible, "an' we'll talk it over."

"Wait," said I. "Who is in command of you?"

"Why, Mr. Pimball, the bo's'n, he'll be in charge of the ship," answered Glibby.

"Very good," I said, "I must talk with him about the future. Do you go on deck, Glibby, and send Pimball below and he and I with the rest of you will soon settle this matter."

"All right," answered the boatswain's mate, turning to the companionway. "Pimball can talk, him an' you can come to terms, I make no doubt."

Now I couldn't allow myself to hesitate for the thousandth part of a second. They say when a woman hesitates she is lost, but in a situation like mine the man who hesitated would have been lost, too. Ostentatiously again I shoved one pistol into the belt that hung at my right side, the other I dropped carelessly into the pocket of my coat, and as Glibby clattered up the ladder, I walked fearlessly, to all appearances, out of the berth and into the cabin, the men giving back respectfully enough to leave me gangway.

"Now what is it that you propose, Master Bo's'n?" I began, sitting down at the cabin table, while the rest ranged themselves about it, some standing, some sitting on the transoms at the sides, as Pimball came lumbering down into the cabin.

For a second he was nearer death than ever before in his life, or ever after but once, as you shall see, but prudence as before held my itching hand.

"We know," began Pimball insolently without further preliminaries, "that this ship's cruisin' for treasure. We know all we'll git out of the cruise is what we signed for an' nothin' more. We've made a good guess that the island lays hereabouts, an' we mean to have more'n our wage. We're goin' to have our share of whatever's found that we're after."

"So you shall," I said, "I'm with you in that. I want something more than my wages, too."

"What's this woman, anyway?" broke out another. "Why should she git it all? She's a mere girl."

"You have said right, mate, who and why indeed?" I answered smoothly, marking him down for my vengeance when my turn came. "Now what are your plans?"

The Island of the Stairs

"We want that 'ere map or chart that you've been seed readin' in your cabin," said Pimball.

Now it happened that I was the keeper of that parchment and of the little stone god. She had appointed me their custodian. No one had sought to steal them, but I kept the chart ever on my person, and the idol in a locked drawer in my berth. I didn't know as to the value of the chart; it might be immensely worth while, it might not. At any rate, it was in a little bag around my neck. I reached down, pulled out the bag, took the torn parchment from it, and threw the two halves on the table. There was not the least use in my pretending ignorance or in refusing to give it up. They could kill me and take it anyway.

"There," said I coolly, "you have it."

Pimball picked it up and looked at it searchingly, matching the halves and scrutinizing it dubiously.

"I can make but little out of it," he said, staring hard at it, and scratching his head, and I doubted if the rascal could read a line for all his assumption of knowledge.

"You can at least see the latitude and longitude on it in the upper corner, can't you?" I asked, hardly suppressing my contempt for the man.

"Aye, that's plain enough," he answered, his face lighting a little as he laid the chart down on the table so that the others might see.

"And you see that little wavy line that runs up from the lagoon over the top of what looks like a wall to an opening in the side?" I continued, determining suddenly to inflame their minds with the treasure so that they would give less heed to other things more important to me.

"Yes, I can make that out, too."

"You see that little mark there?"

Pimball turned around and faced the others crowding about him in great and growing excitement.

"Here, lights here," he growled.

The Island of the Stairs

"The treasure is thereabouts."

The men nearest him shoved forward with their lanterns, illuminating the torn sheepskin as they crowded around, and bent over the table, as I drew back to give them room.

"Aye, I can make that out, too."

The Island of the Stairs

"By—" burst out one hoarsely, "that's the spot."

"What does it mean?" the boatswain asked after a long stare.

"It means, if there is any truth in it, that the treasure is thereabouts."

"What treasure?"

"The plunder of a Spanish galleon."

"An' how did it git on the island?"

"It was buried in that cave there a hundred and fifty years ago by one Philip Wilberforce, an English buccaneer."

"And how come this girl by news of it?"

"The story goes that this Wilberforce was one of her forebears. His ship was wrecked and finally he alone survived. He escaped, was picked up and brought back to England with nothing but the clothes he wore and this parchment in a bag round his neck. With all that he had gone through he lost his mind for a space. He recovered before he died enough to tell some story. His sons quarreled. The story, with one half of the parchment, went to one branch of the family and the other, with the other half, to another. They never got together again until her father and mother, strangely enough the last survivors of the two branches of the family which had been so long separated, came together by marriage, and after their death she pieced out the secret."

I told them the exact truth as you see. How much of it they understood I could not tell. Probably but little, yet the idea of the treasure was real enough undoubtedly and my glib way of rehearsing the story evidently made a great impression on them.

"Is that all?" asked Pimball, as I stopped for breath.

"All that I know."

"And you think there is treasure there?"

Now of late I had changed my mind, why I know not, but I had; yet it would not do to tell them that, for I wanted so to fill their mind with gold as to leave no place for woman.

"I am sure of it," I answered vehemently—"gold, silver, jewels, God knows what, everything to make us rich forever."

"And what do you reckon the value of it all?"

"Oh, several millions of pounds," I answered lightly as if the treasure was so great that a million more or less was of no moment.

To the end of my life I shall never forget the gleaming of their eyes, the covetousness in their faces and their bearing, the tense silence broken only by their deep breathing, the vulgar passion for greed that suddenly filled the little cabin.

"Hurrah!" cried out one old seaman suddenly, and the cabin on the instant was filled with wild cries, bestial, brutal shouts.

As the sound partially died away, I heard the door back of me open. Now I had purposely so placed myself as to be between the crowd and the door. The door was opened but a little way. I was conscious that my lady was at last awake and listening.

"You're the only navigator among us, Mr. Hampdon," began Pimball, smoothly enough, after the men got measurably quiet again, "an if you're really with us, you shall sail the ship there to that island. We'll git the treasure aboard, sail away an' sink her on the South American coast, an' then every man for himself with all he can carry."

"Am I to be captain?" I asked.

"There'll be no cap'n, every man for hisself, I say, but me an' my mate, Glibby, will take the watches in turn. You'll navigate the ship an' whatever is necessary for our safety we'll do at your order. Is it understood?" he went on with a manner that was meant to be ingratiating.

"Yes," answered I promptly, "but under one condition."

"We makes no conditions but what pleases us," said Pimball darkly. "We're masters of the ship, remember, an' this is our last word."

"It is not mine," said I resolutely, yet without heat, for I had yet the hardest part of the bargain to drive and I must command myself if I were to command them.

"Well, it's got to be," continued Pimball with vicious menace, starting toward me with the marlinspike he carried upraised, while others drew their sheath knives evidently prepared to back up their leader.

"Now, my friends," said I, coolly, "we might just as well understand each other. You can kill me if you want to, it would be easy enough, but when you have killed me you have killed your last chance at the treasure. You don't know what latitude or longitude we are in now, there is not one of you that knows enough to take a sight or to sail the ship to the island. You are completely helpless without me. My life means the difference between treasure and no treasure to you. You are all smart enough to see that."

"He speaks right," said an old seaman at the back of the crowd.

"There stands a man of sense," said I, "therefore you will hear my conditions and accede to them."

"Heave ahead," said Pimball roughly enough, evidently not liking the situation but failing utterly to see how it could be amended since I completely held the whip hand of them all.

"What I stipulate is very simple. First of all, I am to have my full and equal share of the treasure with the rest. I am to be treated exactly like the others in the division, and my life and liberty, which are just as valuable to me as yours to any of you, are to be granted me, as I grant those of others."

"Why, we told you that in the first place," growled out the boatswain, "if that's all you've got to say—"

"But it isn't."

"What else?"

"The woman."

"Ah, the woman," said Pimball slowly.

"What had you proposed to do with her?" I asked.

"Why—er I—er," the man faltered, he actually did not dare to say what had been in his mind, and I've no doubt that my pistol never looked bigger than it did when I quietly laid my hand on its butt.

It was probable that the others had not as yet decided what was to be done with her, whatever Pimball may have determined upon. I took advantage of their hesitation and pushed the matter to a speedy conclusion.

"Well," I said quickly, "I want her for myself." Did I hear a groan in the cabin back of me? If I did, I could not afford to hesitate, I could not let them hear. "You saw how she treated me," I cried, raising my voice and banging on the table with my fist; "she struck me, she had me imprisoned. I want her to be given over to me alone."

"But—" began Pimball, not relishing the abandonment of this prize which he had evidently marked for his own.

"I tell you what it is, mates," said I, disregarding him and addressing the rest directly, "I am a poor man and the treasure, or my share of it, means a great deal to me, but revenge means much more. You give the woman to me and I will divide my share of the treasure among the crew."

"Well," began Pimball uncertainly, but the sentiment of the crew under this appeal to their greed was palpably against him.

"Don't be a fool, man," cried the sailor who had spoken before. "Give the lad the wench. When we git the treasure we can buy all the women we need."

"Aye, let him have her!" urged a second.

"He'll bring her to her knees," said a third.

"This very night," added a fourth with a hideous leer and a horrible laugh.

"Stop it," I cried, doubling my fist,—this was no assumed rage either, for my blood was boiling and I could scarce restrain myself longer. "This is my own affair."

The men fell back. They forgot for the moment their advantage in numbers.

"Well, that is agreed at last," said Pimball reluctantly enough, "you takes the woman, we takes the treasure."

"Agreed," said I.

The Island of the Stairs

"Is that right, mates?" he asked of the rest.

"Right O," was the answer.

"It's all settled then," said I, "but no—"

"Bring out the gal then an' let's see her," suddenly began one of the men, stepping forward.

I don't know whether I could have controlled myself any further or not. I rose to my feet, my hand clutching the pistol. The lights danced before my eyes I was so furiously angered. I was about to raise my arm when she saved me. The door back of me was thrown open wide and she stepped out into the cabin. How I thrilled to see her, erect, fearless, more beautiful than ever. She had thrown some sort of a robe about her, and thrust her bare feet into slippers. She had gathered the cloak over her breast with one hand. Her hair was disheveled, but how beautiful she appeared. The men recoiled and I stepped back myself.

"I have heard all," she cried, "you murderous villains, to have killed my captain and seized my ship, and you—you—" she turned to me, "to have bargained for me and to have bought me like an animal, a horse, a dog— Oh, if I had a weapon!"

My pistol was still in my hand and she made a clutch at it, but I was too quick for her. I caught her by the wrist. The spell she had cast upon us by her sudden entrance, her beautiful presence, by her proud, brave demeanor was broken by that touch. The men laughed. God, the remembrance of that laugh makes my blood boil even now.

"I wish you joy of her," said one.

"You'll have a time tamin' her," cried a second.

"Ah, you think so," I cried, determining to carry out the deception to the bitter end and to leave no chance for the least suspicion to arise. I seized her by the shoulders, secretly praying God to forgive me for what I was about to do, and shook her violently back and forth. It was easy enough. A baby in my hands would not have been more helpless. "Silence, you fools," I cried as the men began to laugh again, and then to her, "You belong to me, woman. Do you hear? I've bought you. I am your master. Get back into your cabin. I will have speech with you later." Helpless, amazed, petrified with terror, she could do nothing. I thrust her into the cabin, shut the door and faced the men. "Will you gentlemen leave me alone to tame this she devil for a little while, and I will be on deck presently," I panted out.

"Very well," said Pimball, "but before we goes—" he pointed to a heavy bottle in the rack, "I proposes that we drinks the health of the new navigator an' his lady."

"Right you are," said I, making the best of that situation.

I reached for the glasses that were in the rack and poured out a stiff dram for each man and added mighty little water to it. The room was soon filled with mocking, jeering toasts to my health and happiness. I drank with them. I have ever believed that when you attempt a thing it is better to give your whole heart to it, or you had better not try at all, and I did not propose to spoil the game that had progressed successfully so far, by not joining in. So I drank with the others although I would rather have swallowed poison. They went out one by one, Pimball last.

"You'll play fair with us, Mr. Hampdon," he said earnestly and suspiciously, too, "or—"

"You will play fair with me, or—" I retorted.

"There's my hand on it," he interrupted and I took it, aye and shook it.

"I wish you joy of your woman," he sneered.

"You will see how tame she is tomorrow," I laughed, as he climbed up the ladder and soon disappeared.

My first instinct was to draw the hatch covers and bolt them, but I didn't dare. In fact, Pimball himself kicked them together. I turned to the shut door of her cabin. To throw open the door was the work of a minute. There she stood. She had twisted some kind of a rope out of the sheets of her berth which she had hastily torn in strips. Her purpose was plain. She had intended to end her life by hanging herself from the hook in the deck beam above to which one end of her rope was secured; and she would have done it, too, if I had not come in in the nick of time.

I stared at her for a moment and then reached forward and tore the plaited strands out of her hand and from around her neck and threw them to the deck. It was evidence to me of the deepness of her despair that she had attempted such a thing. It showed me for one thing the excellence of my acting for I couldn't have conceived that she would try to do away with herself if she had the slightest suspicion that I was a true man still. I had convinced even her of my villainy I realized with a sudden pang.

CHAPTER VIII
WHEREIN I MAKE ALL CLEAR TO MY LITTLE MISTRESS

HARD as I stared at her, the glance that she shot back at me matched my own. I never want to see such loathing, such contempt, such scorn on a human countenance again—much less on her sweet face. It cut me to the heart. Conscious of my own innocence of wrong and unaware of the excellence of my acting, I could not understand it for a moment. That she had so far believed my own words against her knowledge of my character and the memory of my long, devoted, faithful service, confounded me. I was appalled, paralyzed for the time being. I didn't know what to say, how to begin an explanation. I stood there gaping like a fool. It was she who broke the silence that was becoming insupportable between us. Come to think of it, the initiative—in speech at least!—was invariably hers.

"A moment," she said wildly, all her feeling in her voice, "and I had done it, traitor!"

"Nay," I protested, "I am a true man."

"You bargained for me, you bought me."

"I was not in earnest," I started to say, but she interrupted me in a perfect tempest of outraged feeling.

"My God!" she burst out, "why didn't you stay away a little longer and I had done it? You villain, you vile, low—"

But at that I found voice again, for I was getting angry myself, my temper naturally being none the sweetest, save ordinarily when she was concerned.

"Hear me," I interrupted in turn.

"Not a word," she said imperiously.

"But indeed you must," I persisted almost roughly, stepping within her cabin and carefully closing the door after me. "It is your welfare alone that I seek. I think you should have known that."

"After the insult on the quarter-deck last evening?" she asked cuttingly.

Now I confess I had forgot that small affair in the graver matters that ensued.

"Never mind that," I began most unwisely.

"Never mind it!" she cried, her face flaming, "I shall never forget your insolence as long as I live."

"Madam," said I, controlling myself again but with added difficulty, "our concern is not with kisses but with—"

"What?"

"Life and—"

I hesitated.

"What else? Speak on."

"Your honor," I said slowly, whereat she stared at my face, now doubtless stern enough in all conscience.

She opened her mouth to speak, but I silenced her with a wave of my hand as I found I could do on various occasions. I did not wish to hear further from her then. What I had to say concerned us both so deeply that I cared not what she said and perhaps that closed cabin into which I had penetrated was the likeliest place for privacy in the whole ship. I could by no means be overheard, so I determined to speak freely and in a way not to be misunderstood. She shrank back against the farther bulkhead as I approached her. Her mouth opened to scream evidently, although she must have realized that a call for help would have but added to her tormentors. But I stopped her before she made a sound.

"I mean you no harm, can you not see it?" I began. "It was all a play."

"A play," she panted, "the murder of the captain, the mutiny of the men, the seizure of the ship, the giving up the chart, your purchase—" she drew herself up—by heaven, she was a brave little thing—"of me," she added, "with your share of the treasure: was that a play?"

"Part of it, madam," I answered, stung by her scorn and stunned again by the thought that she could ever have believed me capable of such baseness, who had loved her, worshiped her, and—but for that fleeting moment when I had kissed her—had ever treated her with such humble consideration and respect.

"Part of it," she repeated, "what part?"

"My part."

"Your part?"

"I am your humble servant now as ever," I said emphatically.

"My master, isn't it, since you bought me?"

"God forbid, I bought not you."

"What then?"

"The right to live and serve you, the right for you to live unharmed, and—"

"And what?"

"And be served by me with no thought but for your safety and happiness."

She stared at me for some moments in deep perturbation and perplexity, her brow furrowed. I had wit enough to be silent and let the speech work.

"Have I wronged you?" she asked falteringly at last.

"As to that, madam," I returned firmly—oh, I yearned to take her in my arms, to press her to my heart, to call her sweet names, but I did not dare—"you yourself must be the judge. But if you will think a moment you will see that I had no other course. What would your fate have been, left to that murderous rabble on the deck yonder?"

"I could have died," she faltered.

"Aye, of course, but not until after they had done with you," I said with a grim plainness of speech, seeing no other way to convince her, and pressing home my slight advantage accordingly.

She shuddered as my meaning became clear to her.

"You should have known me better," I continued a little reproachfully, "than to have suspected—"

"But your insult to me this very night on the quarter-deck and your indifference to it a moment ago!"

Her cheek flushed at the thought of it in spite of herself, and mine flushed, too, or it would have colored had it been less brown, I have no doubt.

"And is a man to be condemned beyond pardon who has served you truly, because he snatches a kiss in a moment of madness and forgets it when your life and honor tremble in the balance?"

"I did not think even you could forget that—ever," she said and I could not fathom exactly her purpose in that remark.

Did she not want me to forget it? Or would she have me remember it? But this seemed like trifling. I turned away bitterly, but she caught me by the arm instantly.

"What are you about to do?" she began. "Don't abandon me now. I believe in you. I see now why you did it. It was to save me and help me. What would I do, what could I do, without you? I am—" she hesitated, it was hard for her proud spirit, and coming nearer faltered out a few broken words. "I am sorry," she finished humbly, with downcast head.

"Say no more," I answered, looking down at the little hand on my sleeve, my soul thrilling to her words and touch. "No harm shall come to you save over my dead body."

"I believe it."

"But that is not enough for me to promise. I mean to extricate you from this peril, to save your life if I can, your honor in any case."

"But how?"

"If the worst came I would kill you with my own hands rather than let you fall into theirs."

"I would welcome death itself rather than that," she answered proudly.

"I believe it will not come to that," I said. "I hope to save you otherwise."

"But is it possible?"

"I think so, I pray so."

"You are but one against so many."

"I have one ally in the ship, you forget," said I, smiling at her, relieved and thankful to see her in her right mind again and awake to the truth and to my real feeling toward her.

"And that is—"

"Yourself."

"A feeble helper," she rejoined, smiling in turn.

"We shall see."

"And will you forgive me for having misjudged you?" she asked pleadingly.

"Gladly."

"My hand on it then," she said, holding out her little palm, which I swallowed up in my large one on the instant, standing silent as usual, holding it the while.

"And are you not sorry that you—you—kissed me?" she faltered at last.

"No," I answered bluntly enough—being a plain man I have always felt compelled to tell the truth—except perhaps when her interests were at stake—"I am not sorry,"—but as she swiftly tried to draw her hand away I added, "I promise you I won't do it again, and you will forgive me, I know. Meanwhile, we have much to plan, we may be interrupted any time, and we had best get at it."

I released her hand and she faced me calmly enough.

"You don't know how much safer I feel when I have you to depend upon," she said.

How my heart leaped at that assurance for I saw by it that she had indeed forgiven me.

"I shall leave everything to you, Master Hampdon," she continued. "Do you tell me what to do and I will do it."

"I know you will. I could not ask a braver, better second," I answered heartily.

At that moment I heard a step on the ladder. Somebody was coming. Quick as a flash I realized the part we had to play in public. I balled my fist and struck the bulkhead savagely. I suppose I must have changed my expression as well for in her surprise, she screamed faintly.

"That's it," I whispered, "cry out again, but louder, louder."

"What do you mean?" she asked hurriedly, with uncomprehending amazement—in this crisis my wits working quicker than hers.

"There is somebody outside. We have a part to play. I am abusing you and you are fighting for your life," I whispered swiftly, then louder, fairly shouting at her, indeed, I cried out, "Down on your knees, wench. You will find that you have met your master now."

I made some sound of scuffling and she did indeed scream loudly. In the midst of the commotion the door was tried, but fortunately I had turned the key.

"Who's there?" I shouted, and to my lady whispered, "beg for help, loudly."

Entering into the spirit of the game and smiling at me since there was none but me to see, albeit she infused strange terror in her voice so that I was amazed myself, she cried at the top of her voice,

"Help! Help!"

I in turn called louder yet.

"Silence woman!" and struck the bulkhead again.

Finally turning to the door I opened it a bit and there stood one of the younger seamen.

"What want you?" I began sternly and stormily. "I don't care to be disturbed just now."

"Well, from the sound of your love makin'," answered the sailor insolently, "I shouldn't judge that you was gittin' any for-ader."

The Island of the Stairs

And here my little mistress showed her cleverness. She had pulled her hair around her face and somewhat disarranged her dress. She sprang to the door and striving to pass my outstretched arm, pathetically begged the seaman's assistance from this great brute, meaning myself! It was well done and deceived the man completely.

"I can't help you," he said. "I'd like to, Mistress, but yon man's bought you with his share of the treasure an' a bargain's a bargain. We must e'en stick to it, though, as I live, I think you worth it," he leered out at her.

"You see," said I speaking harshly to her and thrusting her with seeming violence away from the door, "get back into your corner, curse you!" And then to the man, I said, "Now what's the matter and what's wanted?"

"You're wanted on deck. It is jest dawn. Land's been sighted an' there's a heavy sea runnin'. Pimball an' Glibby want your advice as to what's to be done."

"Good," said I, "I will be with you in a moment. Tell them I have yet a word or two to say to this woman, here."

The man turned on his heel, passed through the cabin and climbed the ladder to the deck.

"Now," I said quickly, thrusting one of my pistols into my little mistress' hand, "we can talk no longer this time; I am going to do my best for you and if I fail here is a weapon. You know what to do with it?"

"Shall I use it on them?"

"No, madam," I answered grimly, "on yourself if it comes to the worst."

"I understand," she said, paling a little.

"Lock the door when I go out and on no account open to any voice but mine."

"I shall remember."

"And keep up the acting," I said, "whimper and cower away whenever we are seen together."

"I shall not forget," she said, standing very straight, looking at me bravely, her eyes shining.

"And now, good-by."

I turned away but she caught me by the shoulder. She extended her hand rather high. I was not so dumb as not to understand what she wanted and so I bent and kissed it, and it was no light kiss of gallantry, but I pressed my lips passionately against the little hand.

"May God keep you," she said, as I turned away, breathing the "Amen" I dared not speak.

I heard the key turn in the lock behind me and with a heart full of misgivings in spite of my stern and resolute purpose, I came out on deck again.

CHAPTER IX
IN WHICH WE ESCAPE TOGETHER FROM THE SHIP

I HAD no idea that it was morning already, the night had passed so quickly. The eastern sky was already gray, and although the day bade fair to be an unpleasant one there was already light enough to distinguish land off to starboard; that side of the ship on the tack on which we were then standing, was to leeward. We had run quite near it in the night. It was still too gray to make out much more than the existence of the land itself, but I thought I saw beyond the nearest island others rising.

At any rate, there it was where it ought to be, and I didn't make any doubt but that it was the island which we had been seeking these long weary months at sea, especially as I recalled the results of the sights which poor Captain Matthews and I had worked out the afternoon before. I felt no little pride in my navigation, by the way. I had told her that I could find it, and I had done so after sailing halfway round the world.

The observation which I had taken then and which I had checked off later, and which Captain Matthews had also checked off by his own shot at the sun, had shown us that we were in about the latitude and longitude of the chart where we might hope to sight land, if the island of our search was not purely an imaginary one. It had not been marked on any chart, to be sure, and I had always felt some doubt about it. The whole story was so strange and unreal, something like a story-teller's romance, that the longer I sailed on the voyage the less real the whole undertaking seemed. With the passing days and the passing leagues I had changed my once confident opinion.

Yet I knew that these parts of the ocean had not been well charted, they were very infrequently visited, and there might well be islands here as well as in other parts of the South Seas that no one knew anything at all about. I had thus sought to reassure myself, and lo and behold, there it was. I was glad then that I had not spoken of my growing doubts to my lady.

Somehow the sight of that land set my pulses beating. If there was land there, why should not the rest of the story be true, why should there not be treasure?

My confidence came suddenly back to me. Yes, that must be the island and the treasure must be upon it. I had professed to give up all of my share to the crew for her—nevertheless, I was not insensible to its value if it were there, and I made up my mind if human strength, human wisdom, human cunning, and unbounded devotion could work it out, I would outwit the crew and get all of it for her, although I realized that riches would remove her at once further than ever from me.

What of it! I couldn't be further from her than I was. She had shown me my presumption and rebuked me properly for it, though indeed she had forgiven me. She was born to be rich and happy and if I could make her the one her friends, old and new, would doubtless make her the other. As for me—well, I could go off on some longer cruise even than this and never come back. Nobody would care. I didn't have much time to think about these things, but the resolution came to my mind then as I set it down here.

The whole crew was on deck. I didn't see Captain Matthews' body about, although I looked hastily for it. I learned later that they had tumbled the poor old man overboard after they had knocked him on the head. He had shot a mutineer before the rest killed him, and he, too, had gone into the sea with the same lack of ceremony— murdered and murderer together to wait the final reckoning. Pimball, Glibby, and one or two others of the older seamen were on the quarter-deck, the rest being strung along the lee rail in the waist, staring at the island. Two good hands were at the wheel. The ship was pitching and laboring heavily and it required two men to hold her up to it.

Everything above the topsail yards had been furled, of course, and during the night they had taken a second reef in the topsails. A whole gale was now blowing. *The Rose of Devon* was a wet ship in a seaway, and she was making heavy weather out of it. Every once in a while a wave would slap her on the weather bow and send a cloud of spray as high as the foreyard, followed by a torrent of water flooding aft. Fortunately it was not cold. We were only a few degrees south from the line so the water was warm and nobody minded an occasional ducking.

I noticed one thing with satisfaction. They had evidently not thought it worth while to break open the arms chest or to force the key from me, which they could easily have done, and therefore none of them was armed. The desirability of getting at the arms had not occurred to them, or else, they being so many, and I but one, they had not thought it worth while. At any rate, save their sheath knives, weapons they had none. Even Captain Matthews' pistols had been thrown over with the body, in their hasty disposition of it.

"Well," I began, as I climbed over the hatch combing and turned aft.

"I sent for you, Hampdon," began Pimball insolently, and his failure to 'mister' me or to give me any title indicated our present relations—and of course I expressed no resentment over his disrespect—"because o' that," he pointed to the leeward toward the island, which we were now sufficiently close to see easily in the growing light, and to which we were rapidly drawing nearer. "What do you make of it?"

"It looks like land," I said to gain time.

"It is land, of course," he rejoined impatiently, "but what land?"

"How can I tell?" I answered evasively. "I have never been in these seas before."

"Well, you took a shot at the sun yesterday, didn't you?"

"Certainly."

"An' where were we?"

I named a latitude and longitude, not exactly what I had worked out but near enough. For obvious reasons I didn't want these ruffians to know exactly where we were or to have any accurate information on any subject. He pulled out the chart as I spoke and compared its figures with those I had given them. Evidently he could read figures if not letters.

"At any rate," he said after studying over the map for a little time, "that ain't far from the p'int we're makin' for, is it?"

"No," I admitted, "not very."

"Do you think that can be it?"

"I can't tell for certain," I replied, determined not to commit myself, "until I get another shot at the sun. I should think the latitude about right, but as to the longitude—"

"An' you can't git no shot at the sun 'til noon, can you?" unceremoniously put in Glibby, casting a long look to the eastward where the sky was thick and cloudy already.

"I can't even get an observation then unless we have clear weather," I answered.

"There'll be no clear weather today, I take it," said an old seaman, standing with the other two.

"I don't much think it," I assented.

"Well, what do you advise, then?" asked Pimball.

"That we stand on slowly during the day and heave to at night, and if we can't get a shot at the sun, stay hereabouts until the sky is clear and the sun visible, then we will know just exactly what course to take and just what's best to be done."

The advice was so self-evidently good, in fact, the only practicable course, that there was no hesitation in accepting it. Pimball, Glibby, and the older sailors conferred together for a few minutes and decided that what I had said was sensible. The boatswain stepped up to the horse block, grabbed the trumpet, and shouted his orders. Presently the ship was hove to with the island well under her lee, distant perhaps a league and a half or maybe two leagues. Personally I should not have hove to a ship so close to a lee shore. I should not have advised it and indeed would have protested against it, had I not suddenly developed a plan, a plan as desperate as ever came into man's head, but then the situation required desperate remedies. And for the accomplishment of the plan the ship was now in the very best position I could have put her.

There were thirty able-bodied men on that ship, not one of whom could have matched me individually, but collectively I was nothing compared to them. If that were the island for which we had been headed, I did not want to leave it without an inspection. Privately I had no doubt but that it was, because, as near as I could calculate from our last observation, it was exactly in the spot where it ought to be, did the parchment tell the truth. As I said before, I prided myself on my navigation and I do still. It was no light thing to sail a ship from England across the whole length of the Atlantic, round Cape Horn and take her up into the tropics and put her just where she ought to be; and I submit that I had a right to be proud.

Well, if that were the island, I was minded to desert the ship with my lady, get ashore and trust ourselves to the tender mercies of whatever natives there were rather than stay with the vessel. The savages, if any there were, couldn't do any more than murder us, and, unless I could shoot her first, the men would eventually treat her, and me too, a deal worse than that. I took no stock in their promises and agreements. Once they got the treasure it would follow that they would kill me and take her. So I made up my mind to desert the ship with my mistress just as soon as I could get away from her, and I thought I could. Rather the natural savage than the civilized one for us both, I decided. That was my desperate design.

When we got *The Rose of Devon* safely hove to, the men all knocked off work at once, leaving the decks in a state of confusion. Indeed, save to clear up the gear, there was nothing to do but wait. Two or three men were stationed on watch and the rest were given the freedom of the ship. I was in doubt as to what to say about the cabin, but strangely enough nobody made any effort to take advantage of the mastery of the crew to quarter himself there. Indeed, their quarters forward were almost as good as ours and they evidently preferred to be together. The ship was generously provisioned and the fare of the men had been unusually good. They did, however, break into the lazarette and help themselves to whatever they liked out of the cabin stores, including a case of bottled spirits.

I looked at that action with very considerable alarm at first, wondering whether it would not be wise or better for me to interfere, lest I should be unable to control them at all when drunk. I decided in the end not to interpose any objections. In fact, I went further in pursuance of my plan and I flatter myself that my design was a brilliant one. From the cabin stores presently I brought out other liquor and let them have as much as they wanted. I even plied them with it, playing the host with much profession of generosity and hearty hospitality. A little liquor would make them ugly and intractable, I reasoned, a great deal would make them drunk, and enough would render them completely helpless. I even joined them in their carousal. It was easy enough to spill my portion and make a pretense at drinking which soon deceived them. They took to the liquor like ducks to the water and voted me a royal good fellow and the prince of pirates. I mixed the raw spirits with very heady wines, too, being much astonished at their capacity, by the way.

The men on watch kept reasonably sober for a time, but even they were not any too abstemious. I saw to that. Later on, the cook, who was not yet too drunk, fixed them up a regular banquet out of the cabin stores, and there was no objection to my taking a portion to my lady in the stateroom below, where she needed no urgent entreaty to keep close and remain out of the way.

My communications that long day with my sweet charge were necessarily much intermitted and very short. I did not dare to be long away from the men on deck. I still wore my sword, and searching through the captain's cabin found two heavy pistols which I carefully charged, concealing them in the deep pockets of my pea jackets. I passed among the men freely, handing out the spirits, opening fresh bottles and bandying rough jests, but took care never to be in any position where I could not command the companion hatch which led to the cabin.

The day did not pass without some altercations and quarrels. One man did endeavor to get below but I was too quick for him. He was one of the most unimportant among the crew and I fetched him a sound buffet which laid him out—he was too drunk to resent it successfully even then—and which was greeted with a roar of laughter by the rest.

"Play fair, Jack," yelled Pimball drunkenly; he was rather better humored in his cups than out, it seemed; "he has give up his share of the treasure for the girl. Let him have her," of which sentiment the rest of the villains apparently were pleased to approve.

The Island of the Stairs

Our drift was slowly but surely in the direction of the island. Indeed, I think we had made half a league or more to leeward since we had been hove to. From time to time I searched the shore with a glass, seeing that the land was protected and completely enclosed by a reef on that side at least, which agreed with the chart; but the sky continued overcast and the mist grew thicker, so I couldn't make out much more than that. It was land and that was enough. It was big enough to support life, and I thought that I detected green patches here and there that betokened vegetation, and if so, there must be water and where there was water there was certainly life.

Nobody took any care to strike the bells, but when darkness fell I declared noisily that I would go below and turn in. All but the most seasoned and hardy drinkers were by this time dead-drunk. There was evidently some little remembrance of my rank, for no one yet conscious made any objection. Pimball, lying supine on the deck, hiccoughed out that he and Glibby, who was in no better case, would keep the watches, so far as the ship needed watching. I ventured to suggest that the ship could be left alone without watch at all under the circumstances and he stuttered out a complete agreement over the bottle which he and Glibby lovingly shared. The wind had moderated somewhat, although it was still blowing hard. We set no more sail, however, and indeed, unless we wished to drift past the island, it was not necessary, especially as they still kept her hove to. With drunken effusiveness they assured me that they would take care of the ship and I went below, having provided all of them with a fresh supply of drink just before.

I sometimes wonder if I would not have been justified in killing them all while they were rendered thus helpless. But I could not bring myself to such wholesale murder, richly as they deserved it and little as I was inclined to mercy. I also thought of clapping them in irons and stowing them below. But there were not irons enough aboard for that purpose and Mistress Wilberforce and I could not work the ship unaided; we could not even feed and water our prisoners. Yet, if I could have counted on three or four true men's assistance, I would have risked it. So far as I could judge the whole crew had become thoroughly corrupt. I did not dare to try any of them. No, to abandon the ship was our only chance.

The Island of the Stairs

How my little mistress had passed the dragging, anxious hours of that awful day you can better imagine than I can describe. And my occasional visits had scarcely reassured her greatly. Yet in an emergency I have never known a woman who had more spirit, who could bear herself more courageously, and I never want to be so loyally or efficiently backed by anyone as she backed me. But I have often observed that it is the waiting that is hardest. It is the standing still and not knowing what is going to turn up, that takes strength out of a strong man and much more out of a nervous woman.

She had left her noon meal practically untouched, and was sitting there in the cabin nervously clutching the pistol, frightened half to death. Poor girl, I didn't blame her. Whatever may have been the cause of it she was genuinely glad to see me when I came in and lighted the cabin lanterns.

"Oh," she cried, "I have been in agony the whole day. Every sound has caused me to seize this weapon and when I have not been watching the door I have been on my knees praying for you and for myself. I do not think I can stand another day like this."

"Please God, dear lady, you shall not," I said, smiling reassuringly at her.

"What do you mean? Have you a plan?"

"I have. The men are all drunk."

"I heard them taking the spirits from the rack, and—"

"I gave them all they wanted, and more," I interposed.

"Was that wise?"

"Certainly."

"I don't understand."

"A little liquor would have inflamed them, a great deal stupefies them. They are as helpless as logs now, and if I had three good men besides myself I could take the ship. As it is—" I hesitated—"I am here to serve you. I am going to leave the ship and take you with me."

"But how—when?"

The Island of the Stairs

For answer I threw open the stern window of her cabin. On a level with it swung a small boat, a whaleboat. Now I had taken occasion during the day to lower that boat little by little, a few inches at a time and then a few inches at another time, as I had opportunity to get near the falls and to manipulate them unobserved, being sheltered by the trunk cabin, of which all the men were forward, and I had succeeded in my purpose without attracting attention, although the risk had been tremendous. Of course, I couldn't lower it clear to the water, but I had brought it down to the level of the cabin windows. Its sea lashings were cast off and I had no doubt, if conditions on deck were as I expected them to be, I could lower it all the way later on with impunity.

"What do you mean?" she asked, staring out of the window and into the empty boat.

"I mean that you and I are going to embark in that boat tonight and leave this ship."

"But where are we going?"

"There is land not a league and a half under our lee. It seems to be the most easterly of a cluster of islands."

"Is it the island we seek, do you think?"

"I have no doubt," I replied, "if there is such an island, that it will be one of the cluster. We are in exactly the latitude and the longitude of the chart if my calculations are correct."

"The island was uninhabited when my ancestor was cast away upon it."

"Yes," said I, "but there may be natives there now, and no savages of the South Seas could be more cruel and ruthless than the men on this ship. To be frank with you, I have no doubt that as soon as they are sure that they have reached the island and that my services are no longer necessary to enable them to find the treasure, they will murder me out of hand."

"And me?"

"They would not be so merciful to you."

"But wouldn't they want to keep you to take the ship back?"

"That is an easy matter," I answered. "All they would have to do would be to lay a course as nearly possible due east and they would bring up on the South American coast, Peru, Chile, somewhere, it would not make very much difference where, so long as it was near Spanish settlements. Then they would divide the treasure, wreck the ship, and scatter themselves and their gains. No, my usefulness ends as soon as they determine that yonder is the island and that the treasure is there."

"Let us go," she said, shuddering.

"I thought you would see it that way," I replied; "the worst the natives can do, if there are any, is to murder us and I shall always save the last shot—" I paused, I couldn't bear to say it.

"For me," she added softly, laying her little hand again upon my arm—and how I loved and prized those little touches, those little evidences of trust and confidence.

I nodded stupidly, speechless as usual.

"What is your plan?" she asked.

"I want you to dress yourself in your stoutest clothes with your heaviest shoes, wrap yourself up in a boat cloak and take with you a few necessaries for your comfort. I will go and rummage the lazarette for provisions, and I will see if I can turn up any more weapons in the captain's room. I dare not go to the arms chest. It is below in the hold anyway, and I can't waste the time to hunt it out. We must hurry."

"Why, you said they were insensible."

"They carry liquor like a line-of-battle ship her tops'ls in a storm," I answered. "They'll recover their senses before we know it. I want as long a start as possible, and indeed I must hasten now."

"Wait a moment," she said. She opened a drawer under her berth and drew out a leather case, which she opened and placed before me. There were two ivory-handled, silver-mounted pistols in it. "They belonged to my father," she said, "with one of them he—he—" her voice broke. I nodded. I knew what he had done with one of them. She rummaged farther and drew out an exquisite sword, quite unlike my heavy one, but if I could judge anything about weapons, of fine temper and strength and with its hilt studded with diamonds. "This was my father's, too," she said, and I recognized it also. It was that I had taken from Arcester. I have worn it many times since in the King's service, for we found it on the ship again, after—but I go ahead of my story!

The pistols were smaller than my huge barkers, better suited for her hand, and to load them from the flasks which accompanied them was the work of a few minutes. I thrust my own heavy weapons back into my belt. I then buckled her two pistols around her waist and bade her have the sword handy also. We might need all these weapons, though I did not think so.

Then I left her and went out on deck. The men were in a profound drunken stupor. Pimball was sound asleep, Glibby was nodding, the lookout aft could hardly keep himself awake and the lookout forward was in much the same condition. The rest of the men were as helpless as logs, like dead men in fact. I made the circuit of the ship. Glibby leered at me as I drew abreast of him.

"Everyth-th-ing a-all-r-right?" he hiccoughed.

"Everything," I answered shortly, "the old barque doesn't need much watching tonight, you can see."

The wind had fallen somewhat and the sea was much calmer.

"W-we w-will g-get a s-s-shot at the s-sun in the m-m-orning," he continued, "an' t-then we will s-s-see where w-we are."

"Aye," said I, "in the morning." I yawned extravagantly. "I will go and turn in, I think. If you need me, call me."

He flung a vile suggestion after me which made me want to turn and heave him overboard, but I had to force a laugh as I went below into the cabin. I saw that in a few moments he and the lookouts forward and aft would be like the rest.

The lazarette was well provided and I stocked the boat handsomely, not forgetting compass, lantern, tinder box, and candles. There was not much water, but I emptied some bottles of wine and filled them, although I did not greatly worry on that account because there would be plenty of water undoubtedly on the island. The boat was provided with a mast and sail. I got into her as she swung at the davits and overhauled spar and gear. Then I shipped the tiller and presently everything was ready. A final search brought to light a narrow locker in the captain's room which I forced open, and found to contain a fine fowling piece, a double-barreled shotgun, and a heavy musket with plenty of powder and ball. These I passed into the boat also, with a sharp and heavy axe.

"Have you got ready all that you wish to take?" I asked my little mistress when all my own preparations were completed.

"A change of linen, some toilet articles and necessaries, needles and thread," she answered, holding up her bundle.

"Good," said I. I judged it was about ten o'clock at night. "Now do you get into the boat, madam."

She had not been on the ship for six months without having learned something about it and she instantly asked me,

"But how are you going to lower the boat away?"

"I will have to go up on deck for that," I said.

"But won't they see you?"

"I don't think so, but whether they do or not, we must chance it, but if anything should happen to me, I'll manage first to lower and then to cut the boat adrift and you will be in God's hands. I don't think they will see me and I am going to do my best to see that nothing does happen, but always you will have to trust to Him."

"I do, I do," she whispered, "and to you."

There was no irreverence in that, I am sure, and I bowed my head silently, assisting her to take her place in the stern sheets. It was not a large boat, yet she made but a small figure sitting there. Then I went on deck. I had a can of oil with me to oil the blocks. It was as I fancied. By that time everybody on the ship was asleep in a drunken stupor and the bottle I had passed to the hard-headed Glibby as I had left him had done its work, too. The two lookouts were sleeping with the others. The man forward was sprawled on the deck. I went forward to make sure. The ship was deserted so far as human supervision was concerned.

Still, I didn't neglect any precaution. I oiled the sheaves of the blocks and lowered the boat away carefully inch by inch until it was waterborne. I reassured my mistress by whispered words as I did so. She had had her instructions, and right well she followed them. She had her boat hook out and fended off the minute the boat touched the water. For me to belay the falls and slide down the forward one, to cast off and take my place in the boat was but the work of an instant. The oars had been carefully muffled. Although the noise of the waves rendered conversation quite safe we neither of us spoke a word until I had rowed some distance from the ship.

As I pulled away I half regretted that I had not poured the remainder of the oil down the fore hatch and set fire to it. But as I said, I could not bring myself to wholesale murder like that, for drunk as they were none could have escaped. No, the only thing I could do was to leave them, though there came a time when I regretted my squeamishness and was sorry I had not made way with them while I had a chance.

We were very silent for the first ten minutes or so. I think my mistress was saying her prayers, while I rowed as I had never rowed before. I could see the stern cabin lights plainly as we drew away from the ship, although for the rest she was in total darkness, no other lights showing, and so soon as we did get far enough away to render talking advisable I had too much to do to spend any time in discussion. I had to get the mast stepped and the sail spread. Fortunately, the breeze was blowing directly northwestward and that was the course we wanted to steer. I suppose it was nearly midnight before we got everything shipshape, my lady bravely helping me with her best efforts, and the little vessel threshed gallantly through the big seas.

The wind had gone down considerably but it was very different on the dinghy to what it had been on the ship and my mistress cowered close beside me, clinging to my arm with that instinctive craving for human contact and for human society which we all feel under such circumstances.

The Island of the Stairs

I had carefully taken my bearings during the day, and as I had a good compass on the boat I knew exactly how to steer. Fortunately the wind held steady. I laid her course so as to clear the northeast end of the island around which I intended to swing so as to be hidden from the ship at daybreak. Of course we would eventually be pursued, but if I could get a long start there might be other islands among which I could choose my refuge. Many things might turn up of which a bold man might take advantage. At any rate, I had escaped from them, and the one I loved sat by my side. The clouds had gone, overhead the sky sparkled with tropic stars. We looked to the Southern Cross and took courage.

We didn't talk much. I didn't dare, and, for a wonder, she had nothing to say. I managed the boat, even if I do say it myself, with great skill. I told her after a while that she was safe. No sound had come from the ship and the lights in the cabin, which at first we could see dimly, presently disappeared. Our escape had not been discovered. I suggested at last that she should go to sleep. I arranged the boat cloak and blankets and although she had to be much persuaded, I finally prevailed upon her to lie down in the boat, her head by my knees, and thus we sailed on through the night.

BOOK III

ON THE ISLAND OF MYSTERY

The Treasure is Found and Fought For

CHAPTER X
IN WHICH WE CROSS THE BARRIER

WHEN day broke I hauled aft the sheet and headed the boat to the southward, for I had now crossed what I took to be the head of the island and could run down the other side. By the time it was fairly dawn I had made enough southing to place the north end of the island between ourselves and the ship. My calculations had been remarkably accurate again. I had weathered the islands fairly in good time, and now as the sun rose I steered the boat directly toward the land, the changed direction of the morning breeze permitting me to lay the desired course.

My hopes were high and I felt a kind of exhilaration at our escape, although I was by no means inclined to minimize the possibilities of grave peril we might soon be compelled to meet. The island was our destination, however, and for it therefore I determinedly headed my small craft with its precious and still peacefully sleeping cargo. Poor girl, if ever a woman needed sleep and rest it was she. And her easy slumber pleased me the more for it bespoke not only weariness amounting to exhaustion but confidence and trust—and in me, and I was stirred to even greater devotion.

I had sailed in nearly all the waters of the globe, frequented and unfrequented, and I fancied I had chanced upon most of the odd things to be seen therein, but I am free to admit that the island was unlike any I had ever looked upon. The chart should have prepared me for it, but it had not. In the first place, like most Pacific islands, this was enclosed by a barrier reef over which the waves broke in white caps as far as I could see. I supposed that somewhere there would be an opening in the reef through which we could sail, although the chart, rather roughly drawn, had showed none. That an opening should exist was so invariably the case with all such islands as I had ever known or read about that I counted upon finding one here. But I could not see any opening from the boat as yet. The lagoon enclosed by the barrier reef seemed to be from a half to three-quarters of a mile wide.

The strangest part of the whole game was that the island itself looked like a whitish-gray wall rising straight up from the lagoon for, I suppose, from one hundred and fifty feet in the lowest parts to three hundred feet or more in the highest. And the wall appeared to be without a break. It stood up like a solid rampart of stone, its top covered with greenery.

From where we were situated at just that moment I couldn't see on to the end of the island, although from my inspection of it the day before, I judged it might be six or eight miles long, and as I had sailed past it I estimated it was about the same breadth and nearly circular in shape.

A long distance away on the other side and hard to be seen at all from the level of the sea in the small boat in which we were, lay other islands, faintly outlined on the far horizon. I doubt if I could have seen them at all had not the rising sun smote full upon them. They were too far away for my purpose, which was to make a landing as soon as possible and find some concealment or, at worst, some practical place of defense. I therefore paid no attention to them, not realizing what a part they were to play in the adventure following.

I suppose I must have threshed about somewhat when I brought the dinghy to the wind and changed her course, for presently my little mistress awoke. She sat up instantly and after the briefest acknowledgment of my good morning and the briefest reply to my inquiry as to how she did, she stared at the land toward which we were heading in so far as the wind would allow. It was a bleak, inhospitable looking place, that gray rough wall, in spite of its infrequent cresting of verdure, I will admit, and she too found it so. After she had stared hard at the land, she cast an anxious glance to leeward, but of course could make nothing definite of the distant islands there.

"We have made good our escape from the ship, since she is not to be seen," she began.

"For the present, yes."

"Do you think that they—"

"They'll be after us, of course, as soon as the drink wears off."

"And when will that be?" she asked anxiously.

"This afternoon probably, but we've nought to fear from them for hours yet," I reassured her.

"Well, Master Hampdon, what do you propose between whiles?" she said.

"We must get ashore," said I, "as soon as possible. By the time their debauch will have worn off, they will either bring the ship here or send the boat after us. Afloat we can do nothing, ashore we may find some concealment and probably make some defense."

"It is a forbidding looking shore."

"Aye," was my answer, "but any haven is better than none, and it may prove better than it promises on a nearer view."

"Have you seen any evidence of human life?" she asked, nodding in acquiescence to my proposition.

"No," I replied.

Indeed, not a curl of smoke anywhere betrayed the presence of mankind. Had it not been for depressions on the top of the wall here and there, which were filled with vegetation, one might have supposed the island to be nothing but a desolate and arid rock, but this reassured me. I thought it strange that there was no mountain or hill rising from beyond the top of the wall, but I was yet to see how strange the island was. Indeed, I think there can be no other like it in the world. For I have inquired of many mariners and they all confess that they have seen nothing anywhere that in the least resembles it. Some, in truth, seem incredulous to my tale, though I set down naught but what is true.

But as it was full morning now, I decided that first of all the creature comforts had to be thought of. I offered to relinquish the tiller and prepare something to eat, but Mistress Lucy took that upon herself. What we had was cold, but there was plenty of it, and at my urging she ate heartily. For myself I needed no stimulus but my raging hunger. I wanted her to be in fettle for whatever might happen and myself too, and so we fed well.

We had not much conversation the while, but I do remember that she did say she had rather be there alone with me than on the ship, whereat my heart bounded, but I had sense enough to say nothing. Her loneliness and helplessness appealed to me. I might have been bold under other circumstances, but not now. She was dependent upon me and I could not bring myself to the slightest familiarity, so I only answered that I would be glad to serve her with my life and I prayed God that we might come safely out of the whole business, to which prayer she sweetly added her own amen.

Well, we coasted along that barrier reef a good part of the morning until we reached the other end of the island, and discovered to our dismay that there was absolutely no opening, no break in it through which we could make our way. When we reached the lower end, my lady was for sailing around on the other side to seek farther, but this I did not dare. We had heard nothing from the ship or her boats, and I did not propose to arouse any pursuit by coming within possible range of her glasses. I did not know where the *The Rose of Devon* lay; for aught I knew, they might have put her about and she might be off the south end of the island. It was better to let sleeping and drunken dogs lie, I said. After my rather abrupt negative of her proposition she watched me in silence as with clouded brow I pondered the situation.

"Madam," said I at last, "there is naught for us but to try to go over the reef in some fashion. As I scanned the island yesterday through the glasses I couldn't see any opening in the reef on that side, and although I never saw or heard of a case like this before, I make no doubt but what the reef is continuous and there is no access to the island except over it. And come to think of it, Sir Philip's chart showed no opening either."

"I recall that the reef completely encircles the island on the little map," assented my lady.

"Then we must even pass over it as we can. I have had some experience in taking a boat through the surf, and although it is a prodigious risk I believe I can take this one over. For one thing, this dinghy is built like a whaleboat; we may capsize it, but it is practicably unsinkable. I propose to take a turn of the painter around your waist. If she goes over you will not be thrown completely adrift. I am a stout swimmer and can catch the boat and haul you in it or on it, and whatever happens our lives will be preserved."

"Will it be so very dangerous?" she asked me.

I could have minimized the danger, of course, but I thought she was woman enough to hear the truth. She might have to face even greater dangers presently and she might as well become accustomed to the idea sooner or later. So I reasoned, and therefore I told her.

"I don't see how the danger could possibly be greater, and yet," I added, "I think we shall win through if you will sit perfectly quiet and trust to me."

"I will do whatever you tell me," she said, with a most becoming and unusual meekness. "I think—I know—I trust you entirely, Master Hampdon."

"Very well," said I quietly, "and now may God help us."

Fortunately, the tide was making toward the shore of the island. I selected a spot where the huge, rolling waves seemed to break more smoothly than elsewhere, which argued a greater depth of water over the barrier, less roughness, and fewer possibilities of being wrecked on the jagged points of the coral reef. Dousing the sail, unshipping the tiller and rudder, and pulling the oars with all my strength, after an unuttered prayer, I shot the boat directly toward the spot I had chosen. Just before I reached it, I threw the oars inboard, seized one of them which I wished to use as a steering oar and stepped aft past my lady, who sat a little forward and well down in the bottom of the boat. I braced myself in the stern sheets and waited. We were racing toward that reef with dizzy speed rising with the uplift of the wave. I had just time for one sentence.

"If we die," I shouted, "remember that I have been your true servant always."

She nodded her head, her eyes glistening, and then I turned to the business in hand. A huge roller overtook us. The little boat rose and rose and rose with a giddy, furious motion. Suddenly it began to turn. If it went broadside to the reef and a wave caught it or one broke over it, we should be lost; but I had foreseen the danger. I threw out my oar and with every pound of strength in arm, leg, and body, I thrust blindly, desperately against the heave of the sea.

It was an unequal combat, a man against the Pacific Ocean. I could not have maintained it for long. Yet the few seconds seemed hours. The strain was terrific, of all the tasks I ever attempted that taxed my strength the most—save one, as you shall see. If the oar broke we should be lost. It bent and buckled but held like the good honest piece of English ash that it was. Sweat poured from me, my heart throbbed, my pulses beat, my head rang. It was not in human power to continue. I was about to give way and let go all when I cast one glance at my mistress. I saw her pale face, her bright eyes staring into mine. My strength then was about gone, but that look of appeal, entreaty, and confidence nerved me for one last supreme effort.

There are not many men with as little experience in that sort of work as I had enjoyed who could have done what I did, for I held the boat steady, her bows fairly and squarely pointed to the reef in spite of the thrust of the ocean, and I thought triumphantly that I was going to make it safely in spite of all. I reckoned without my host, however. The wave we were riding broke just as we reached the top. We sank down into what seemed a valley of water, the breakers roared in our ears, the spray fell over us like rain. We sank lower and lower, there was a sound of grinding along the keel. We had struck the coral evidently. The boat stopped a moment, motionless.

Unshipping my oar, I thrust it violently at the reef. The blade caught in the coral. I put all my weight against it. The water rose, the trough of the sea into which we had fallen suddenly filled. I clenched my teeth and closed my eyes and thrust again. The boat lifted a little, moved a little, the keel grating along the reef. I heard a scream faintly and opened my eyes. I caught a fleeting glimpse of my lady's face, but could give her no attention. I struggled desperately to drag the oar free. The coral rock into which I had jammed it held the blade like a vise. The boat rose and moved faster. The oar was wrenched from my hands. The inrushing wave and the moving boat passing reef together, the great sea finally broke upon us.

We were over, but the wall of water struck the boat, now broached to, full on the beam. She was lifted up, whirled over and swept inward. The mountainous sea struck me on the back and side, knocking the breath out of me and fairly hurling me clear of the boat so that I fell into the boiling water alongside. My lady had half risen as the boat swung broadside to the sea and she was also swept into the water. If she had remained crouched down she would have fallen under it and probably would have been killed.

The sea rolling inward swept us toward shore. It was well that I had taken precaution to pass the painter about her waist and tied the lashing securely. For by means of it she regained the overturned boat and climbing up clung to its keel in comparative safety for the moment. I, on the contrary, was driven landward and away from her. I struggled desperately, half-dazed, to regain the boat. I might better have attempted other things, but to see my shipmate there on the overturned boat, so drenched and forlorn, maddened me, and I fought flooding tide and flooding sea to reach her.

I could not call out, I was too spent and breathless for that, but I struggled on and on. Whatever the cause, the wave which had so nearly undone us was followed by a succession of the hugest rollers I have ever seen. Usually the waters inside such reefs as we had passed are smooth and calm, but on that day they were scarcely less rough than the ocean. To attempt to make head against them was vain.

I know now that my lady called to me to desist, seeing from her more elevated position on the boat's keel that we were rapidly being driven toward a strip of sandy beach. But I did not hear. I did not become aware of our nearness to the shore until my foot actually touched bottom.

The next wave carried me landward and left me prostrate on the sand. I scrambled to my feet and leaped to meet the boat, also being rolled toward the beach.

The Island of the Stairs

"Then she bent over me."

Mistress Lucy had cast off the lashing and had let herself into the water, and none too soon, for the capsized boat, I think her mast catching on the bottom, was suddenly righted by the waves, the mast carrying away, and before I could avoid it I was struck by the prow and knew no more.

By this time, as I afterward learned, my brave shipmate had got to her feet in the shallows. She saw the boat hurled upon me, saw me borne backward on the beach, saw me carried up the sand, and left lying senseless by the spent wave.

With feelings which she did not attempt to describe until long after, she ran to me, and with a strength, the source of which she could not explain, dragged me further up the beach. I am a large man and with all my inertness and the weight of my sodden clothes, I know not how she compassed it.

Then she bent over me. I did not ask her what she said or did until she chose to tell me later of her own will, but I presently awoke to find her looking into my face, holding my shoulders with her hands and frantically calling me by name.

"Master Hampdon! Master Hampdon!"—her voice rose into a scream of terror.

"Fair and softly, my lady," I answered slowly, sitting up and looking about me. "I am dizzy, my head aches from the blow, but I believe there are no bones broken. Let me see," I continued, rising and steadying myself by a great effort by the boat, which luckily enough lay quietly on an even keel bedded in the sand near by, and unhurt save for the broken mast. "And you, dear lady?" I asked as soon as I could command myself.

"Safe, safe, thank God and you!" she cried tremulously.

"Nay," said I, trembling from the violence of my efforts at control, "give to Him alone the glory."

But she shook her head. I reached down my hand toward her and lifted her up and for the first time got sight of her. She had worn a dress of some silken stuff, over a petticoat, or skirt, of darker, heavier, woolen cloth. Her overdress had been torn to rags by the sea. There was a great rip in her underskirt, which she caught on a nail or splinter when she slid from the boat into the water. Both her buckled shoes were gone and one stocking had been stripped from her by the seas. Her little bare foot gleamed whitely on the golden sands. Her hair was undone, water dripping from her sodden raiment.

Under my steady inspection she colored violently and instinctively sought to conceal that bare foot beneath her tattered clothing. She hath protested often since as to how she must have looked, but to me then as ever, she was beautiful in her disarray and disorder and as to her sweet, white foot I longed to kiss it; aye, and take no shame to myself in this confession, either. And I have done so since, not once but many times.

Obviously the first thing was to provide her with clothes. She had her other apparel in a little chest which I had lashed to the thwarts, but when I searched for it in the boat it was gone, and the thwart too. The weight of it and the final buffeting had wrenched both clear. In fact, the boat was swept clean save for the weapons, which I had thrust under the thwarts and lashed there, and the contents of the lockers. Even the sail had been dragged clear of the boom which still clung to the foot of the broken mast.

The sea had gone down a little and as I stared out across the lagoon I caught sight of the sail. Fortunately it had got foul of the broken thwart, which had been wrenched loose by the drag of the box that had been lost, and it was still afloat. It was a light canvas. It flashed into my mind that it would do. Without a word I plunged into the lagoon and a few strokes brought me to it. I dragged it ashore and spread it in the sun before the inquiring gaze of my shipmate.

"What is that for, a tent?" she asked.

"Your clothes," said I. "The first thing for me to do is to turn cobbler and tailor. You couldn't go about, like a South Sea islander, bare armed and barefooted," I continued calmly. "Out of the sailcloth we can make you some sort of a dress."

"But my shoes and stockings," she said facing me bravely, although the color came and went at the untoward situation for a modest maiden.

"I can manage the shoes," said I, "but the stockings—" I paused. "When we have made the dress," I continued "you won't need that red skirt and you can make shift to slit it into lengths and wrap them about your legs. They will protect you better than what you have lost."

The Island of the Stairs

Fortunately I brought along with me a sailor's needle and palm with stout thread aplenty still safe with other contents of the lockers. It was intensely hot in the sun and it did not take the canvas spread out upon the sand long to dry. Picking it up we moved inward across the narrow strip of beach to the cool shadow of the cliff. There was much to be done, but clothes and footgear for her had to be attended to first of all. And as we had seen no one, we went about making them with energy and a good heart.

Here my little mistress could help. I am as good a tailor, I dare say, as any man that sails the seas, but feminine rigging had never been my experience or endeavor. Between us, with the aid of my sheath knife, which I ever kept sharp, we managed to cut out a plain loose dress like a tunic. Fortunately, she being but a small woman and understanding how to use all the goods to the best advantage without wasting any, we were able to get out a suitable garment which fell below her knees halfway to the ground.

While she was busy cutting it I had taken off my vest or jerkin of stout leather, and with her remaining shoe as a model for shape and size, I contrived the sort of a foot covering that the savages of North America call a moccasin. It was shapely enough too, and I made the soles of several thicknesses of leather, and protected the heel and toe by additional strips. So I managed to knock together a very serviceable pair of loose shoes. By the time I had finished them my lady had got her pieces laid out, and the sewing of them devolved upon me, for she could by no means with her small hands manage the rough cloth and large needle. I worked hard and before noon I had the garment fit for her to wear.

My mistress then retired behind the protecting rock and donned the tunic. She had taken my sheath knife with her and had made herself some kind of a girdle which she had cut from her now useless skirt. She had put on the shoes, and with further strips from the cloth had replaced the stocking that she had lost, and the other one also. She must have seen the admiration in my eyes as she came rather timidly forward to my gaze. I suppose she had some doubts as to her appearance, but my tailoring and cobbling became her vastly, I avowed. The canvas was new and white, the scarlet about her waist, even the brown leather of my moccasins with the red above, added a charming touch.

From a woman of the world and society she became in one hour, it would seem, a creature of simplicity, like the ancient Romans of whom I had read. She still possesses that garment and those shoes, and sometimes in the privacy of her chamber she dons them for me. The sight brings back old days and brave days of hard fighting and true comradeship and great adventure on that far-off island set in that tropic sea under those blue skies. And I love her better than when in the diamonds and powder and silk and brilliant array with which nowadays beauty obscures itself under the demand of fashion.

CHAPTER XI
HOW WE EXPLORE THE WONDROUS SHORE

"THANKS to you, Master Hampdon," she began, reassured by my glance, "I am now clothed and shod comfortably and in my right mind."

"You are always in that, Mistress," said I quickly.

"You did not think so in the cabin of the ship," she laughed, and giving me no time to answer, for I am not quick at speech on some occasions, as you who read must have noticed, she ran on, pointing to the barrier reef as she spoke, and staring at the breakers smashing against it, "but shoemaking and dressmaking are small things after what you did out there."

"It was nothing," said I.

"I watched you. I was not too frightened to do that, and there is not another man on earth who could have brought me over the fearful maelstrom of water to safety here."

Well, that is true, why not admit it? I thought.

"Not many white men," I replied, glad for her praise, "but natives in their canoes aplenty."

"But a canoe is light and easily managed, not like this heavy boat."

"No, I admit there is a difference"—as indeed there was—"but now we must think on the future," I added.

"And what is to be done next?" she asked.

The next thing to be done, I decided, was to overhaul the boat. I pulled the plug out, drained the water from her, hauled her up on the sand above high water mark, my lady helping me as if she had been a man. I remonstrated with her about it, I begged her not to do it, finally I even ventured on a command to which she paid not the least heed.

The precious powder and shot we found dry and safe in the flasks in the air-tight lockers. From the same safe place, we got some hard bread, some cold salt beef, and with water from a brook that gushed out from under the rocky wall and ran across the beach we broke our fast again on this plain rough fare. It was not yet near noon, but we had gone through much since that early breakfast, and were healthily hungry again—and so we made our meal. Dry, hard eating to be sure, but we were thankful to God that we had it.

Finishing, and feeling much refreshed, we decided that our first duty was to explore the island to see if there was any break in the cliff wall, and if there was any access to the inward parts in which I hoped to find vegetation, trees, and the delicious fruits with which I knew the tropics abounded. My lady was heartily in favor of such a course, and we at once set about carrying it out.

A hasty survey assured me that the cliff was of coral formation, jagged and broken into many a crevice and cranny. If we were hard put to it, I was sure we could find a cave in which to pass the night if it were necessary. After we had made out what we could, I suggested to Mistress Lucy that we start at once exploring, proposing that we follow the course of the sandy strip and find out what we could of our island refuge. And, so, taking with us some provisions, for we might have to go clear round the island, and our arms, we presently started out. My mistress professed herself well rested and ready for anything. My own endurance was not yet at its limit, and I felt the necessity of discovering the lay of the land at once, in view of the presence of Pimball and the ship in those waters.

Yet I felt very easy in my mind regarding any present peril from the ship, for I knew that no boat she possessed could run the reef as I had done, and even if she had had another like the dinghy I was confident that there was no man aboard her that had the strength and skill, to say nothing of the courage, to bring her through. Indeed, for all my skill and ability we ourselves had only got through by the favor of God. If there were no natives or wild animals to be feared we were at least safe for the time being. I explained this to my companion as we trudged along the hard, white sand, whereat she was greatly relieved and her quick mind being freed of apprehension turned to other things.

"Think you, Master Hampdon," she said, "this is the island of which my ancestor wrote?"

"I am sure of it," I replied.

"He referred to it, if I remember right as *'Ye Islande of ye Staires,'* did he not?"

"Yes," was my answer. "You remember he indicated a stairway about the middle of the island."

"Surely, if we are to get to the top of yonder wall it must be by stairs of some sort."

"It would not be difficult to climb it," I assented, "for a man, that is, save for one thing."

"And what is that?"

"Those pinnacles of rock are as sharp as needles. It would be like climbing broken glass. The climber would be cut to pieces before he had gone halfway. See," we approached the wall closely and I pointed out to her how sharp the edges were. "If it were granite rock these ridges and splinters would be weatherworn and smooth, but this coral formation is of a different quality."

"Then if we find no stairs we are in a bad situation," she said thoughtfully, examining the towering wall.

"There must be stairs," I answered, "or there must be some other way. The latitude and longitude agree with your ancestor's description, and I make no doubt we shall chance upon them."

"But if there are none?" she persisted.

"Doubtless we'll find some break to let us up or in," I answered easily, evasively it may be, but hopefully, not being minded to pass our existence on the narrow strip of sand on which we were walking.

So we tramped along, searching the shore and sea and finding nothing. After perhaps an hour's monotonous going, when we had traversed about a third of the distance of the island, we rounded a projection of the cliff and there before us—rose the stairs!

Now I know that you who read will accuse me of fond invention, yet I have not the wit or the imagination of the romancer. I can only relate the facts as they were. What we saw was a gigantic stairway, irregular, but made of huge blocks of roughhewn stone—not coral rock, but harder stone of firmer texture, like granite almost. I was not familiar with the stone either. There was no symmetry about the stairs. Some of the stones rose perhaps three feet, and others not more than as many inches, but stairs they certainly were, and they surely had been made by man. The stones were most carefully fitted, being laid up without mortar, the joints so close that I could scarce thrust a knife blade between. The huge blocks were of monstrous size, too; much too great in bulk and weight to be handled by any but mechanical means. I never could conceive how natives or primitive men could have shaped them, moved them, and finally laid them up in the form of stairs. I have since made inquiries of learned men and find that for all their study they, too, are at sea as to who were those mighty builders and how they built.

Nor did the stairs alone awaken our amazement and quicken our curiosity. They ended in the circling belt of sand, here a little wider than elsewhere. At the bottom on either side, two gigantic statues, or busts, of stone had been erected. Their bases were buried in the sand and they rose to quite twice my height above, and I am good six feet tall and more. These stones were carved into the rough yet not unreal likenesses of human faces. The carving had been done with marvelous skill considering, and the faces were not of the native type either. They were of our type, only distorted and exaggerated. The carving included the breast; one was a man, the other a woman. They were made of the same hard pinkish rock as the stairs, and the angles and projections upon them apparently had been softened and smoothed by hundreds of years of exposure to the weather. They were not unfamiliar to us either, for they were, making due allowance for size, just like the little image Sir Philip had brought back. They had the same enormous sightless eyes, the same long protruding jaws, the same hideous fang-like teeth, the same repulsive features. We looked at them both, experiencing a perfectly natural and understandable feeling of horror and disgust. One had lost his crown, but the other was intact as he had left the carver's hands.

The very size of them intensified our disquiet. They were caricatures of course, but withal they were intensely natural and lifelike and not less wonderful than the stairs, over which for centuries they had been the silent watchers and guardians.

Certain I am that you will find it difficult to credit these marvels, and will dismiss them perhaps as a traveler's idle tale, yet I have given you the latitude and longitude of the island and you may go there and see them for yourself if you desire, and you may perhaps find what treasure we left there, too, for a reward! When you return you can testify that I lie not, but speak the sober truth.

Why we had not discovered these stairs from seaward was because they did not come squarely down to the water's edge at right angles to the wall, but instead lay, as it were, parallel to it in a niche within the wall, so that they were somewhat sheltered from observation from the sea.

As we broke upon them suddenly, therefore, Mistress Lucy clutched my arm. We naturally drew together at the sight of such gods, or devils, in stone.

"The giant stairway!" she cried in thrilled amazement.

"It is indeed," I said triumphantly, as I realized what our discovery meant, "just as it was stated in the parchment."

"And the great stone faces," she added in a voice in which there was a note of horror.

"They, too, were mentioned, you remember," I said, striving to speak cheerfully, though I was deeply impressed myself.

"And just like the little one back in the ship."

"The very same," was my reply.

"They were very old two hundred years ago," she commented.

"Aye, it appears to me that they must have been old a thousand years ago, or more," I assented.

"Could those stairs have just happened that way? Or did someone build them, think you?"

"Yes," I replied, "those are the work of men, skilled men, too, for they are too regularly laid up to be by chance."

"Yes, of course, and the images could never have come there by chance," she admitted.

"Certainly not, but let us go nearer and ascend them," I said, taking her hand and leading the way, and she was so preoccupied that she did not notice.

I observed, as we approached the stairs that the rock had been worn smooth by the wind and weather, or maybe by the passing of many feet, and the steps were quite practicable for ascent. The angle at which they rose was sharp, too.

"What is on top, think you?"

"I know not."

"Wild men or savage beasts?" she faltered.

"The parchment said naught of animals or permanent inhabitants of this island," I reassured her.

"No, that it did not," she assented.

"Well, then, let's chance it."

I had thrust the pistols in my belt, save for the one she carried, and had the musket in my hand. I looked to the priming of them so that I could depend upon them in case of an emergency, although I confess I did not expect anything to happen. Save for the sound of the wind and waves and our own voices the place was pervaded by that sort of deadly stillness which indicated the absence of humanity, or even the larger forms of animal life. Except for the birds of gorgeous plumage and the gulls and other sea fliers I believed we were absolutely alone on the island.

Then we began the ascent. It was easy enough for me, but hard for her, and several times I made bold to lift her up the higher steps, which she suffered without comment or resistance. She told me long afterward that my manner toward her then and thereafter had been perfect. I had determined in my heart to show her that although I could snatch a kiss on the quarter-deck of a crowded ship, on an island, alone, I could treat her with all the courtesy and consideration of the very finest gentleman of her acquaintance.

The Island of the Stairs

When we at last reached the top, before us lay a broad pathway rudely paved with the same hard stone. This road led straight across the top of the wall toward the interior of the island, of which we could see as yet nothing, because the wall hereabouts was covered with dense, luxurious vegetation and seemed of great thickness, perhaps a mile or more, as we found as we traversed the way. Progress was difficult even in the pathway. It would have been impossible in some places but for my heavy cutlass with which I cut a path where the place had become overgrown by trees and bushes which had forced their way through the cracks, overturning and breaking the heavy flagstones and blocking up the path, which, it was evident, had not been traversed for generations; perhaps not since the old buccaneer himself had walked along it beneath the spreading trees.

There was naught for it but to continue along the rude paved way, for it was impossible to penetrate the jungle on either side, even if we had desired it, and once more looking to my weapons, one of which I kept in hand, although I was sure now we should not need them, and had indeed nothing to fear, we followed the ancient way. For perhaps a mile we pursued our journey across the top of the wall, winding in and out among the trees, through the jungle, the path evidently seeking the most level direction, for the top of the wall was very much broken and irregular.

At last we came to an open spot on the inner edge overlooking the whole island, and before us lay such a picture as few eyes, at least of our race, had ever looked upon. The wall ended abruptly and fell downward, on the inner or landward side, as precipitously as it rose outwardly and to seaward. Before us lay a most entrancing valley, perhaps three or four miles across, and maybe half as long again in the other direction, and which was walled about in every direction. It was sunk beneath this wall crest for perhaps one hundred feet or more. In the center of the valley the land rose a little higher than the island wall, making a very considerable hill, tree crowned on the slopes, but largely bare save for more images, on the crest. Through the valley ran a brook which ended in a little lake, which I suspected had some subterranean connection with the ocean. As far as we could see, and the whole circuit of the island was now clearly visible to us, the enclosing wall was unbroken. The valley was filled with clusters of trees and alternating stretches of grassy meadow. Why it was not completely overgrown with trees I could not imagine. Perhaps the ground was too shallow in places for trees to grow.

We would have been hard put to it to descend the wall to the valley, but for the fact that the same people who built the stairs that gave access to the wall from the sea had also built a similar flight which made the descent to the valley possible, indeed easy. Before we essayed the descent of the stairs, we drank our fill of the beauty and mysterious charm of it all. Indeed, there was no sound that came to us except the twittering of the birds, of which there were many brilliantly plumaged flitting in the trees. All else was still, lonely, deserted, oppressively so in fact.

I was constrained to think of our situation as we scanned the lonely prospect in silence. A man and a maid cast away upon an absolutely deserted island rising from the most unknown and unfrequented seas on the globe, seemingly with no chance on earth of escape therefrom. The one possibility of getting away, *The Rose of Devon*, worse than useless to us because of her evil crew. What were we to do? What could we expect? Suppose we found the treasure, of what value would it be to us?

I cursed myself for my weakness in allowing my lady to come upon this voyage of death and disaster. I wished that I had destroyed Sir Geoffrey's letter. And yet as my glance fell upon her my thoughts changed. A man and a maid, I have said. Distinctions of rank did not exist in the Garden of Eden. This was the world's first morning again, and by my side, dependent utterly upon me, stood—Eve! My heart beat, my face flamed at the thought. Here, if nowhere else, she might—

"What think you of this?" my lady broke the silence, and she broke more than the silence, for her words recalled me to my better sense again.

"I do not know," I answered, shamed in my soul at my imaginings.

"Is it not like the crater of an ancient extinct volcano?" she ventured.

"No," said I, "these are coral rocks and there is no sign of lava about them, yet it has somewhat of the appearance, especially that flattened hillock in the center."

I have since talked with many men and studied the writings of the most learned geologists, and from what I have been able to glean from them, and the suggestions I have been able to give, it has been fancied that perhaps the rocky projection in the middle of the valley, where later on we saw the great altar of sacrifice with its attendant idols, was the original island which was once surrounded by a coral reef now become a wall, and that some great upheaval had lifted the whole up out of the water in ages gone by, and that the barrier reef over which we had passed was the second attempt of the busy little insects to surround the island again. And indeed, though I know but little about such things, the theory may well be true, although it gives no solution of stairs or images or altars. It seems easier to explain nature than man, you see. But these things, naturally, did not occur to us then.

"What is to be done now?" asked my little mistress.

"I hardly know," I answered, staring at the green cup of the island, encircled by the white walls, like a great emerald wreathed in pearls. I should not have thought of that comparison, myself, but it occurred to my lady later, and she told me, so I have put it in to embellish this rather dry narrative of mine. "I see no signs of human life or of animals, except birds," I continued, "I firmly believe that we are absolutely alone on the island."

Involuntarily, I looked at her as I spoke, whereat she came instantly toward me without hesitation.

"We are alone," she said, as if divining my thought, "and I am in your power. I am weak and you are strong, but—"

"Madam," said I, with all the formality I could infuse in voice and bearing, "you are as safe with me as if you were in your late father's arms, and surrounded by all the people you love."

"I know it and I trust you," she answered. "Indeed, indeed, Master Hampdon, I am glad to be here, to be away from that awful ship of death and I believe this is the island which we have been seeking.

The Island of the Stairs

Where else in the world is there such a wall and such a flight of stairs? I am sure the treasure will be here and when we search for it we shall find it."

"Very likely," I answered, "but what is exercising me most now is, first of all, what is going on in that same mutinous ship, and next how we shall finally get away from here."

"You are impatient," returned my lady, smiling.

"Impatient for you, madam," I interrupted, checking myself from further self-revealing speech just in time.

"One thing at a time," she continued. "By the favor of God, we have escaped from the murderers and mutineers and by His providence we have come safe across the reef. We shall not starve upon this island, and I have no doubt that sooner or later you will devise some means for our escape. You have done so well so far that I feel quite confident; in fact, if Captain Matthews were with us, I should feel almost happy."

This was rating my power very highly I knew, and I felt that I might not be able to justify her confidence, but if I failed it would not be for lack of trying. It was long past noon by this time. I made sure of it by looking at the sun and confirming it by my watch which I most carefully kept running during all our sojourn on the island, which indicated close on six bells, three o'clock. Our talk of the ship recalled me to myself.

"I think," said I, "that we had better postpone the exploration of the island until another day, and go back to our landing place. If I know the men on that ship they will guess that we have escaped to this island, and they will bring her round to this side, where we may have them under view and they us. And I shall feel safer and more confident and comfortable in my mind about your future if my present doubts as to her whereabouts be settled."

"Think you that they can come at us?" she asked, in sudden alarm.

"I think not," I answered confidently, "but still, to make sure, I should like to have them under observation."

The Island of the Stairs

Well, to make a long story short, we retraced our steps over the broken path until we reached the stairs on the other side. The descent of them was much easier than the ascent, and by four of the clock we stepped on the sand again. There before us in the offing was the ship.

We saw her people quite plainly and I doubt not they caught sight of us immediately also. They were scarcely a third of a mile away from the reef, perilously near, I thought, and we could mark them crowding the rail and staring landward. We could see them brandishing their weapons and we could imagine the yells which must have arisen from the decks when they caught sight of us.

I stared at them indifferently enough, but not so my little mistress. She shrank closer to me, her face paled and I had all I could do to keep from throwing my arm about her shoulders. I blessed God that she was here on the island and that I was by her side, and that neither of us was on the deck of the ship.

CHAPTER XII
INSIDE THE REEF WHICH WAS AT ONCE PROTECTION AND PRISON

THE ruffians aboard the ship did not content themselves with simply staring at us, for presently they assembled on the port quarter, the ship was under all plain sail on the starboard tack at the time, the wind having fallen to a gentle breeze during the day, and clambered into the cutter swinging at the davits. As she was lowered into the water fully manned, Mistress Lucy drew even closer to my side, seizing my arm with both hands.

"Let us fly, they are coming to take us!" she cried in great alarm.

"But they are on a vain errand," I reassured her calmly.

"But why? How can you know that? Oh, Master Hampdon, let us hasten away."

"We have a protector," I answered confidently enough.

"God?" asked she.

"His handiwork," I replied, as I indicated with a gesture the barrier reef over which the waves were breaking.

"But we passed it."

"Yes, in a light dinghy and you remember the difficulty and danger. They will never surmount it in that heavy cutter. They will not even attempt it, when they have seen it nearer, trust me."

"But if there should be an opening?"

"I don't believe there is one," was my reassuring reply. "We know that there is not one on this side, since we examined it ourselves, and my careful inspection yesterday did not reveal any on the other, and with that conclusion the chart agrees, you remember. No, I have no fear that the crew of *The Rose of Devon* can get at us."

"And we can't get to them," she answered more composedly.

"I have no wish so to do," I laughed.

"You don't understand me," she persisted, "what keeps them out, keeps us in."

"Yes," I admitted, "that is true, but for the present I don't mind being kept in, so long as they are kept out."

She looked at me quickly and confessed afterward that my words begot some quick suspicion which she admitted was unworthy of her and unwarranted by any act of mine, but I looked so placid that it soon passed from her mind. As a matter of fact, I had not appreciated the significance of my words. I should have been perfectly willing, I should be still, to pass the rest of my life alone on that island, or anywhere else with my lady only. She was company enough for me and although we have ruffled it bravely together since then, and have even borne our part with dignity at the King's court, I am happiest when she is by my side and no one else is near. I was happy then. I had got her to myself; my little mistress must look to me for everything. The haughty queen of the quarter-deck was now the humble dependent of the lonely island.

I did not know what dangers lay before us, what perils encompassed us. I could not foresee how we were to escape from the Island of the Stairs, for so we had named it. Those thoughts did not trouble me much. I had brought her safely from a ship filled with mutineers, pirates, and murderers; I had landed her safely on the island despite circling reefs and raging seas; the future could take care of itself. Sufficient unto the day was the evil thereof—aye, and the good, too!

We trudged along the sand parallel to the course of the boat which was following the outward edge of the barrier reef seeking what I knew they would not find, an entrance to the lagoon and thence to the island. The lagoon narrowed in places, until, had it not been for the roar of the waves on the barrier reef, a hail could easily have carried. I am ashamed to say that I used insulting gestures on occasion, whereat some of them stood up in the boat and shook their fists in our direction.

I shall confess to having taken much delight in irritating them until Mistress Lucy implored me to cease. Thereafter we watched them in grim silence and contempt. Although I was sure they could not reach us, their presence was nevertheless a menace and a barrier to us.

After they had rowed the length of the island they gave it up and went back to the ship, which had followed their course.

By this time the day was far spent and night was at hand. We retraced our steps and came to the place where I had hauled up the dinghy. I now observed with some pride that both the shoes and the dress I had made for my lady would serve their purpose. Meanwhile we both were hungry. The provisions we had taken with us we had eaten during the journey. The next business was supper. I had noticed some cocoanut trees and other strange tropical fruits, so I had no fear of starvation. We could live on the island indefinitely, therefore I was not sparing with the provisions. Feeling need of something warming we kindled a fire with flint, steel, and tinder from their case in the locker, and made shift to boil some coffee. We had neither milk nor sugar, but the taste of civilization did us good, and our refreshment added to our encouragement.

For the night I capsized the boat and drew it close against the coral wall, spread a spare sail I found in the after locker and her boat cloak which had drifted ashore and dried out during the afternoon, upon the clean, dry sand, and bade her take her rest. It was snug, dry and comfortable.

"But you?" she asked.

"I shall do very well here with my heavy jacket and I shall lie across the stern of the boat, between it and the cliff, out of sight but within touch or call if you need me."

"I am afraid," she said softly.

"Nothing can come to you except over my body and I am a light sleeper. A touch, a word will arouse me," I said reassuringly.

"I would not have you harmed, either," she persisted.

"I shall not be."

"There may be wild beasts."

"I do not think there is an animal on this island," I laughed, "and we have seen no signs of man. The ship certainly would have attracted the attention of someone had not the island been deserted."

"But those men out there?"

"You forget the rampart that God has flung about us. Now, madam, you can go to sleep in safety, I assure you."

"Before that," she said, dropping down on her knees in the sand and motioning me to follow her example, which I did awkwardly enough—I hope I was not a mocker or disbeliever, but I confess that I did not often bend the knee then—"we will have a prayer together."

She had slipped a little prayer book within her bodice and she now drew it forth from her canvas tunic and by the light of the fire read the Psalm of David which begins, *"Out of the deep have I called unto thee, O Lord, Lord hear my voice."* And then she prayed, using some of the old collects of the Church and adding one of her own making, in which she besought God to care for us further, while she thanked Him for having raised up a defense for her in my poor presence, I listening very humbly and saying a heart-felt "Amen" at the end.

I shall never forget that scene; the gray cliff towering high above us, its crest lost in the darkness, the overturned boat, the white-clad woman kneeling by the fire, its light playing upon her until her face looked like the face of an angel, myself further back in the shadow. It was a dark, moonless night but the stars shone with tropical brilliance and in our ears echoed and reëchoed the crash of the mighty waves upon the barrier which was at once our prison and our fortress. There was a silence for a little space when she had finished and in that silence I devoted myself before God to her service again, and then we rose and she gave me her hand.

"You have been a true knight and gentleman," she said softly, her eyes shining, "and I thank you."

I could only take it dumbly and stare at her, whereat she smiled brightly, although her eyes suddenly filled with tears.

"And now," she added, "God keep you. Good-night."

I then kissed her extended hand, which she suffered without resistance.

"I will leave you for a little space," said I, "and so good-night and God bless you, too."

When I came back she was snug in her place under the boat. I sat for a long time before the fire, thinking and making plans for our escape. The ship did not give me much concern because I was sure she could not come at us, and in the end she must go away and leave us alone with the treasure, maddening as that might be.

It was a strange fortune that had brought us here. How mysteriously things had worked out. The marriage of her father and mother, the last representatives of the two lines that had come from the same ancestor but had been separated for a hundred and fifty years, which had brought together again the old story of the island, which had been handed down from father to son, and now to only daughter, during those many years, with the tradition explaining it; the indifference with which her father, Sir Geoffrey, had received it, his leaving the parchment and the image to her after his death, the discovery that her mother years before had given her the other part of the chart; the saving of the two thousand pounds by worthy Master Ficklin from the great estate which had been dissipated by her father; my own opportune appearance on the scene—I had returned from an American voyage a short time before his death— her consultation with me; her determination to take the money she had and charter a ship; our securing *The Rose of Devon*, the enlisting of the crew and the starting off on this wild goose chase, and what had happened since—I recalled them all.

At first believing, I had come latterly to scoff at the whole matter, and had at last laughed to myself at the prospect of finding an island or treasure, and had discredited the story of the old rover buccaneer who had captured the Spanish treasure ship, his own having been sunk in the encounter. Now I could reconstruct the whole scene. He had manned the galleon with his own crew and they had been wrecked on this island reef—if this were the island—but the sea had subsided, and filling the boats with the treasure they had hidden it in a cave on the other side of the wall. The sailors had lived there for some years, but had finally been attacked by some natives, probably from the islands I could see dimly on the horizon, and they had all been killed except Captain Wilberforce, who had feigned madness and become tabooed.

He had escaped in a canoe from the other islands, whither he had been carried, and had fallen in with a Spanish trader, after what voyaging and suffering who could say? He had been trans-shipped from one vessel to another and finally reached his home, a harmless madman on that subject his friends and neighbors and even his family thought, with the parchment, the image, and the tradition which he bequeathed to his two children after he recovered his wits before he died. They had quarreled, married apart, and lost sight of each other. And here we were, a hundred and fifty years or more after the death of the old Elizabethan buccaneer, on his very island. Was the treasure there still, where the tradition said he had placed it? We should see. I now believed that it was.

A long time I sat there until I finally threw myself down and fell fast asleep. I must have slept a long time and soundly for I was wearied. It was she who awakened me. When I opened my eyes and saw her sweet face bending over me and heard her dear voice calling me, I declare I almost felt as if I had died and gone to heaven, and was being welcomed by an angel. But that was only for the moment. I realized everything at once. She herself had but just arisen.

Our first waking thought was for the ship. She was still there in the offing. She had been hove to during the night. I could imagine what fierce debate and wrangling there had been aboard her. The fact that we had landed would convince them that the island contained the treasure for which they had committed murder, and which they could now by no means come at. And that we had escaped them, cozened them, and now could be seen on the beach braving them, in no way diminished their anger. Even if there were no treasure, they would be anxious to get possession of us and wreak their vengeance upon us.

The day that passed was much like the afternoon before. Although we were by this time persuaded that the reef was an absolute protection, a vague possibility that they could devise means to pass it in some way, kept us uneasy on the sand. We must have them under observation. We were eager to explore the beautiful vale enclosed by the huge rampart, but we did not dare to be where we could not watch the ship. We did walk along the shore and ascend the giant stairs in the afternoon. Then while she watched the sea within calling distance of me, I managed to penetrate the jungle with axe in hand, so that finally I made shift to cut down a cocoa palm tree and we gathered as many delicious nuts as we could carry and returned to the shore. And we made plenty of conversation easily during the hours of watching.

On the ship we had conversed mainly about business. Now we had no business and my lady was pleased to look at me in some surprise as I told her what I guessed about the formation of the island and displayed unthinkingly the knowledge of the South Seas and other parts of the globe which I had acquired in my long studying and wide cruising.

"Why, Master Hampdon," she exclaimed, opening wide her beautiful eyes, after I had explained to her something of the nature of the island and how I thought it had been made and the use of the great quantities of fruits thereof, "you seem to know more than any of the finest gentlemen I have ever been thrown with."

Whereat I was flattered beyond measure and showed it, but she was kind enough not to rebuke me for my foolish vanity. And indeed there were not many—perhaps even none at all—among her acquaintance who could have done for her what I had; they were men of spirit, in truth, but they lacked my experience and my strength.

That night the sun set amid lowering clouds. With a sailor's weather sense, I was sure that we should have a storm. Pimball and Glibby sensed it too. We could see them making things snug alow and aloft on *The Rose of Devon*. They were good enough seamen, as far as that goes. The wind, if it came, would be offshore, and there would be no danger of the ship being driven upon our reef, but there were islands to leeward which they seemed to have forgot but which I remembered. If it came to blow hard I would not want to be in the position of *The Rose of Devon*, even if I do prefer a ship to the shore in a storm, but I want plenty of sea room and that the poor little *Rose of Devon* had not. I surmised that the attention of the crew had been so persistently fixed upon us that they had scarcely ever glanced to leeward even.

The Island of the Stairs

I explained all this to Mistress Wilberforce as I made things snug for the night. She would be perfectly protected by the overhang of the cliff and the overturned boat, and I showed her, before I left her alone beneath the boat, that the same overhang of the cliff would protect me from the wind and the rain if the storm broke. And so after prayers again and a long look seaward we went to sleep.

About midnight, so far as I could judge, I was awakened. The storm broke with all the suddenness and intensity of the tropics. Such peals of thunder and such flashes of lightning I have never witnessed although I had been in many storms throughout the world. To sleep further was impossible. Mistress Lucy came out from her boat and stood beside me as we leaned against the cliff while the storm drove harmlessly over our heads.

We could see the ship at intervals by the vivid flashes of lightning. She was making fearful weather of it. She was always a wet ship and the huge waves fairly rolled over her. Once she went over nearly on her beam ends and I thought she was gone. I did not view her position with a great deal of regret, either. Although she could not come at us, she was a terrible menace. But the next flash of lightning showed that her main topmast had gone by the board, or had been cut away, so she righted. Presently she drove off before the wind with a rag of her foretops'l still showing, and that was the last we were to see of her, we thought.

Praise God, that was not true after all!

CHAPTER XIII
IN WHICH WE ENTER THE PLACE OF HORROR

STORM bound under the lee of the cliffs, we passed long and anxious hours the next day, although our only misfortune was in the inclemency of the weather which kept us close and prevented our further exploration of the island and a search for the treasure. We were completely sheltered and we had plenty of the refreshing milk of the cocoanut to vary our other food. Nor did we neglect to improve the rainy hours by much pleasant converse and by further work upon my lady's tunic and shoes. Also I made her a sort of hat out of palm leaves which she could tie upon her head by further strips from that invaluable and seemingly inexhaustible skirt of hers. And I made myself a head covering of some of the cloth, letting it fall low over my neck, as I had observed the Arabs at Aden do, it being there that the fierce heat of the tropic sun centers its attack—at least I have heard so.

The second day after it began the tempest finally blew itself out, although the great surging seas still broke tremendously over the barrier reef and the spray shot a score of feet or more above the crests of the highest waves. It was only the reflex of the storm, however, for during the night the wind had subsided into a gentle breeze. All was calm and peaceful; nature never looked so bright and smiling, it seemed to me, as at the dawn of that eventful day.

When we scanned the sea early in the morning there was of course no sign of the ship. I imagined that the hazy islands dimly seen in the bright sunlight on the far-off horizon could tell a tale of sea disaster if they would. Any way, I did not believe that we should ever see *The Rose of Devon* or her crew again. In both those beliefs I was mistaken, as you shall find out, if having read thus far, you have patience to continue until the end.

Our first inclination, and there was none now to intimidate us, was to mount the stairs again, cross over the wall once more and look for that cave. We had neither chart nor record left, we had but our memories to trust to, but we were both agreed that the cave lay in the inner wall, and that the parchment said it was the central one of three adjacent openings which gave entrance to the treasure chamber.

Now I had noticed that the great coral wall, both on the outer and inner sides, was honeycombed with openings, rifts, fissures, and caves which, by the way, were more frequent and deeper on the inside face; why, I knew not. We should have been hard put to it to decide where the cave lay, and should have been compelled painfully and laboriously to search the whole face of the cliff in its extent of fifteen miles or so, but for the further direction of the parchment. I remembered that, sailorlike, old Sir Philip had given us a bearing. How did his words run? Something like this my memory told me:

Toe fynde ye mouthe of ye tresor cave take a bearing alonge ye southe of ye three Goddes on ye Altar of Skulles on ye middel hille of ye islande. Where ye line strykes ye bigge knicke in ye walle with ye talle palmme, his tree, bee three hoales. Climbe ye stones. Enter ye centre one. Yt is there.

Plainly, our first duty was to descend into the enclosed valley and explore the hillock in the center. I made no doubt but that we should find some sort of an altar and more of those curious and hideous stone images there. If they still remained, the rest of our task would be comparatively easy.

With this determination, therefore, we set out. As I did not know how long our exploration would require, and as I rather thought we should have to make a day of it, we started betimes after a very early breakfast; indeed, as we invariably retired shortly after sunset, we naturally rose at break of day. I took along food enough for the day, knowing that we could get water from the brooks, and fruit which I judged would be good for us from the trees.

We went directly to the stairs, mounted them, and stared about us in amazement. The storm had been a frightful one. We had not been able to estimate its power from where we had been sheltered on the lee side of the island, but here the uprooted trees and the wide swaths cut in the jungle on the top of the wall showed its terrific force. I had no need for my axe. There were cocoanuts upon the ground and other fruit which would all rot away before we could consume a hundredth part of it. Within the shelter of the island cup, as we were presently aware, less damage had been done, still even there the ravages of the tempest were widely manifest.

Delaying but little on the top of the wall, we crossed it rapidly and finally entered the valley. It was with a feeling of awe that we stood for the first time fairly within the vast cup at the foot of the inner stairs, completely shut out from the world by the great towering rampart of rock which entirely enclosed us. I had never felt so far removed from the world as then. Outside, of course, the limitless ocean ran beyond the barrier reef, but one could follow it unto the dim, far-off distance with his vision; within the cup the glance fell upon the rocky wall on every hand. It was almost like being in a prison, for all its tropic loveliness. It was strangely still, too. There was no wind down where we were. We could no longer hear the ceaseless splash of the breakers on the barrier. The calm must have been like that of the world's first morning, when God walked in the garden and saw that it was fair. We were alone in it too. Ah, this Adam dared not look at this Eve, lest he should find her all too fair.

Beneath the trees and quite invisible from above, a paved road or path, barely wide enough for four to walk abreast, extended straight across the island to the hillock in the middle, while smaller paths seemed to follow the course of the walls on either side. The ground was gently rolling, and the road, though overgrown in places and badly broken, was in much better condition than the broader path on the top of the wall. I suppose the fact that it was sheltered protected it. We passed along it for a mile and a half without much difficulty; as usual, hearing nothing, except the breeze in the palms and the birds in the thicket. We went in silence mainly. We had so far progressed in good comradeship that talking, unless we had something especial to say, was not necessary. And the stillness about us did not move us to speech.

Finally we arrived at the foot of the hillock. As I observed from the wall, it was grass-grown and palm tree clad. Indeed we should have been hard put to it to have ascended it, so dense was the vegetation, had it not been for the fact that the path was continued around the hill constantly mounting. Where it ran the somewhat shallow earth

The Island of the Stairs

had been cut away on the hillside, and the rocky surface laid bare. Of course, this path was frightfully overgrown, and rendered further impassable by the trunks of trees which had fallen across it; some, from their freshness, probably cast there by the storm of the night before. We managed it, however, and as our identification of the place of the treasure depended upon our reaching the crest of the mound, we were compelled to climb it or give over the search. Leaving most of our baggage behind, including my coat, for the day was now hot, we began the ascent.

We went on with the utmost care. I cautioned my lady that she must on no account move recklessly. A broken leg or a sprained ankle would place us at a terrible disadvantage, and be a most serious hardship, and she must avoid the possibility at all costs. I assure you I was equally careful of myself, too. It was intensely hot under the thick shade of the trees where the breeze had no chance to penetrate, and I was sweating mightily when I finally drew my companion, her face bedewed almost as much as my own, up the last steep ascent and stood upon the crest.

We could see now why the top of the hill had seemed level when we first looked at it from the wall. Indeed, the coral rock rose in a kind of sharp, bold escarpment eight or ten feet above the adjacent tree tops, making a sort of tableland or platform. This level, probably artificial, had been paved with the reddish-gray rock of the stairs and statues, and pathways and trees, perhaps artificially planted or more probably the result of Nature's sowing, grew here and there in open places in the pavement. I may say in passing, that in all our exploration of the island, which however was not very thorough or complete owing to our limited stay upon it, we saw no quarry whence this hard, pink rock could have been taken.

The only satisfactory solution was that it had been brought there across the seas by the makers of the monuments and stairs, whoever they might have been. They must have had large, seaworthy vessels and adequate means of land transportation, to say nothing of a most considerable engineering ability to accomplish these mighty works.

Well, the level top of the hillock was in shape a parallelogram, in extent perhaps an acre and a half. It was the most curious place I have ever seen. In the middle of it, with its four sides parallel to the sides of the plateau, was a huge stone platform or altar, perhaps one hundred feet long by seventy feet wide. Completely surrounding this altar, some distance away from it so as to make an aisle perhaps ten feet in width, rose a line of huge statues carved, like those at the foot of the stairs, into the semblance of monstrous and repulsive human faces. I judged that some of them were at least thirty feet from mid breast to the top of their crowns. Not one of them was like another. There was variation in each just as there is variation in human faces.

All were ugly and horrible, namelessly evil, but all were lifelike and were, singularly enough, European. Yet that a European could have carved these statues was beyond the wildest possibility. I have since thought, and others have thought also, that perhaps the primitive men who erected that altar to some unknown god might have been men of the same racial stock as ourselves way back in the dim days of the world's first morning.

At any rate, these statues or images rose at the breast from a kind of terrace a foot or so above the level of the platform, paved as elsewhere. They formed a sort of cloister or colonnade around the central platform which rose twenty or twenty-five feet above. A few of them had fallen down, but the more part were standing as their carvers or builders had left them. On the center of the raised platform or altar, stood three more of the same monster busts, placed one after another, the largest one being in the middle. They were in line, all looking in the same direction which my pocket compass told me was somewhat to the north of northwest by west. They were staring, therefore, into the general direction of the setting sun.

At the front, or west, end, the great platform was approached by a flight of steps. The stones of the pavement were so cunningly fitted together that only here and there had a seed lodged and grass-grown, except where the palm trees had sprung up, breaking the pavement. The stones of the platform or altar and the approaching stairs were also laid up without mortar and fitted in the same way. How savages with probably nothing but stone knives could have so perfectly trued and fitted the surfaces of such huge stones, to say nothing of moving them at all, was, I confess, beyond me; but so it was. The altar was in good repair, indeed so massive was it, and so well made, that nothing short of an earthquake could disturb it.

Standing so high, the fierce winds that swept over the plateau and platforms had probably assisted in keeping it clear of vegetation, of anything in fact, for save for the few scattered palm trees, it was as bare as the palm of my hand. And indeed, cleaner, for although my lady had brought with her some soap, I, not knowing how long we should be on the island and realizing her dainty habit and what a deprivation it would be to her to be without it, refrained from using it and cleaned myself as well as I could with water and sea sand, a poor substitute for soap as you can well imagine.

Well, we stood upon the platform and surveyed the scene in silent awe. Nothing in the parchment had led us to suspect all this, although I recollected the mention of the stone faces looking toward the niche under the big palm tree, the spot in the wall by which we were to locate the treasure cave.

"Come," said I at last, breaking the silence, "we will have a nearer look at these gentry."

"It seems like the temple of a vanished race," breathed my lady softly, staring about her in growing wonder.

"Aye, and of vanished gods," said I, extending my hand.

There was something weird and eerie about the plateau and we felt better for the warm touch of each other's hand; at least I did. I always felt happier when I touched her little hand, but in this instance the feeling was somewhat different. In a certain sense it seemed like profanation for us to be there, yet we went on steadily, if slowly. We passed by the colonnade of statues, around the inner platform, and deliberately mounted the stairs.

Something, I know not what, made me bid my mistress pause before we reached the top, and I looked to my pistol, and loosened my sword in its sheath as I did so, although why I did so, and what I anticipated, I cannot say. At any rate, I mounted to the top alone. There before me lay a platform which was sunk beneath me for a depth of two feet and which was surrounded by a low wall on the top of which I stood. The three images rose from a smaller platform on a level with the top of this wall in the midst, and the whole place was filled with a horrible and frightful mass of human bones. Skulls, legs, thighs and smaller bones heaped in terrible confusion lay bleaching before me, and the space between them was filled with a fine dust, doubtless the dust of earlier bones which had moldered away through centuries. Those that still preserved their shape were the top layer and were bleached perfectly white. They lay in all directions as if they had been cast aside carelessly and at random, yet there were indications that there had been a path from where I stood to the platform of the three images, which platform I perceived was just about wide enough to lay a human body on it at the base of the first image.

I stared apprehensively, I must confess, at this frightful charnel house of the centuries. The only evidence of humanity we had discovered on that island were these bleached and moldering skeletons. I would have prevented her, but my mistress suddenly came up and stood by my side. Then I thought she would have fainted as the full horror of the scene burst upon her.

"Men have been here," she faltered, "horrible, cruel men."

"Yes," said I, "but centuries ago. Look, the bones are bleached white. You have naught to fear."

"Let us leave this frightful place," she whispered.

"Presently," I answered, "but you will remember the directions of the chart. I must stand upon yonder altar and get my bearings. The treasure cave should be in line with the statues and a niche or depression in the wall on the further side."

"Yes," she replied, "I remember."

"Well then," I said, "will you go down to the platform out of sight of this horrible place and wait for me there?"

"No," she answered nervously, "Master Hampdon, wherever you go I must go. I can never be left alone upon this island."

I tried gently to dissuade her, but, as usual, she would have her way so that at last I gave in perforce.

"Well then," said I, "at least let me go before."

I stepped down into the great receptacle meaning to clear the way with my feet by kicking aside the layer of bones, and, on my extending my arm behind me with both her hands caught in mine, she followed me down into the enclosure. Of course we had to walk upon the broken remnants of humanity, but I thrust aside as well as I could the larger pieces and skulls, and she, I afterward learned, followed with her eyes tightly closed, trusting entirely to my guidance. Indeed she clung to my hand with all the nervous strength and power she possessed.

So we finally reached the platform. I lifted her up on it and followed myself. We were not the first human beings who had been lifted to that ghastly platform, I was sure, and as I stood there I could hear in my imagination the protesting, shrieking, struggling captives about to be immolated. I could close my eyes and see the blood dripping down the sides of the altar, as the breast of the bound victim was pierced with the stone knife and his beating heart torn out and lifted up in the face of these devilish and horrible gods by the terrible priests of the ghastly sacrifice. It required little effort to reconstruct the fearful cannibalistic orgies on the platform below, in honor of whatever awful deity they worshiped. I did not let myself dwell upon it, nor did I say anything about it; and my mistress knew too little about such matters in her sweetness and innocence and purity to have such thoughts as mine—thank God!

I led her carefully around the altar platform therefore, until we could stand at the rear end by the side of the line of statues and look across the island. Sure enough, there was the niche or depression in the wall which Sir Philip had mentioned, although the "bigge palmme tree" was gone, or else lost amid hundreds of trees like it. Beneath it, careful scrutiny showed a rough pyramid of stone leading up to what seemed to be openings in the cliff wall.

So far every detail in the old buccaneer's parchment was absolutely correct. I was certain now that the treasure was there, and that we could find it. And a certain exaltation filled me. At least, we had not come upon a fool's errand, though what good the treasure would do us in our present case after we had found it, I did not stop to consider.

"See," I pointed out to my little lady, "following the edge of the three statues here with your eyes, the nick or break in the wall of the cliff is right in line."

"I see," she said.

"And below it," I continued, "for your bright eyes are perhaps keener than mine which have looked into the salt seas and over the glare of water blazing in the sun for so many years, what can you make out?"

"I see above the tree tops what looks like a pyramid-shaped heap of stones, the stones of which Sir Philip spoke, perhaps."

"Yes," I replied excitedly, "and at the top, at the apex, what?"

"There is a darker opening in the wall between two others."

"The treasure will be there," said I confidently.

"Let us go to it," she shuddered, looking about her. "I don't wonder that Sir Philip came back a madman if he lived for long in the presence of this."

"We have nothing more to do here," I answered, as I led the way to the edge of the low altar.

I leaped down and then turned to help her. She was very white and I thought she was going to faint. I don't blame her, the surroundings were so terrible. I acted promptly, reaching up and taking her in my arms and carrying her as if she had been a baby; and indeed she was no great burden for me. Her head dropped to my shoulder. I did not know whether she had fainted or not. Her eyes were closed. I ran swiftly across the enclosure, descended the steps and without hesitation turned to the edge of the cliff. I stopped there, cursing myself for not having brought any water, but as I stopped she opened her eyes.

"You are safe," said I gently, setting her on her feet again, "the horrors are all behind us. See, there is before you naught but the beautiful greenery of the island, and—"

An expression of gratitude came across her face.

"Let us go down," she replied. "We must never come near here again."

"Please God, no," I repeated, as we retraced our steps down the cliff and along the winding path, Mistress Lucy gaining strength and color as we passed at last out of sight of the hideous platform.

CHAPTER XIV
WHEREIN WE FIND THE TREASURE

IT was necessary to retrace our steps along the path to the foot of the great stairs in the island wall. There were treeless meadows here and there on the way, where we rested, and a lovely brook of cool, delicious water where we broke our fast, though it was not yet noon; but the openings or clearings all stopped before they reached the foot of the outer wall which was almost hidden in vegetation. I remembered the paths which had led off on either side from the stairs, too. We followed one to the north easily enough. It was not like the highway over which we had just come, being only partially paved, although it had once been thoroughly cleared, and the rise of the wall was such that it was still practicable. We turned to the right, plunged beneath the trees and pressed resolutely on, keeping as close to the main wall as possible.

This wall to our left was dotted with openings of caves, but none of them seemed to fit the description we carried in our memories. The undergrowth deepened and grew denser as we progressed, and finally I had to open a way with my axe. The tangled masses soon gave way before my sturdy energy, and at last we entered a considerable open space which extended to the wall. There above us were the three openings beneath the depression in the crest; surely enough, the one in the middle being greater than the others. I deemed that the entrance would be high enough to admit me, who am much above the usual stature, without bending my head. It was elevated halfway up the surface of the cliff, and the only approach to it was by the great heap of stones, not laid up with the order and regularity of the giant stairs, but apparently piled together haphazard by people unskilled to make any other practical way of ascent.

It was difficult enough for us to climb just as it was. The heap of stones evidently had not been mounted for years, and the stones had broken and fallen away in many places. Indeed, we had to rebuild the pile here and there, which entailed some hours of arduous labor on my part, in which my lady would participate until I laughingly threatened to take my belt and strap her to the nearest tree unless she desisted. Whereat, smiling strangely, she stopped and, sitting down near by, watched me at work in silence.

Reaching the top at last we stood on a shelf in front of the cave mouth. I peered within but could see nothing but the blackness. When we left the ship we had taken a lantern and a few candles, you remember. I had brought the lantern with me that day. We now lighted it with the flint and steel and tinder and stepped silently in. My lady followed me close, being, as she had said, unwilling to be left alone, and ever ready to face any peril in my company.

Above the low entrance the cave wall within rose to a height of perhaps twenty feet, making a vast vaulted chamber with Gothic suggestions about it, for the coral, before it hardened, had been built into curious shapes and fantastic figures. We did not notice this so much at first, for with a wild shriek, my gentle companion suddenly caught my arm and pointed downward.

The floor, like that of the central altar on the hill we had just left, was covered with human bones, a gruesome sight for anyone, and certainly for a woman, and made more gruesome because of the dull lighting of the cave. These bones also were bleached white and had evidently been there a long time. We could scarcely take a step without treading upon them. I had all I could do to keep my mistress from running back toward the mouth and thence to the ground and it was not until I had reassured her again and again that she would consent to go on further.

As we had been compelled to pass on by our desire to get our bearings before, so if we were to get the treasure we would have to suffer this now. I think if it had not been that her previous experience on the hillock had somehow given her some confidence, my lady could not have endured this sight, treasure or no treasure. But she was a brave woman and when I urged that we were not to be balked in our search of thousands of leagues by dead men's bones which, though horrible, were after all quite harmless, she summoned her courage and we went on.

As our eyes became accustomed to the light, for indeed the candle lantern cast but a dim radiance over the vast apartment and the entrance was so small comparatively that little daylight came

The Island of the Stairs

through, we saw off to the right against that side of the cave the same kind of an altar built of the same stones as on the hill, though much smaller and surmounted by a similar image as ugly as the others, though nearer the human size. Bones of human beings, men, women and children I judged from the difference in sizes, lay before it, and there were heaps of bones on the floor around it. It came across me that it was another altar of sacrifice, and that the worshipers had also been eaters of flesh—cannibals! For I reasoned that in that island and especially in that dry cave, the bodies of the sacrificed would have been dried up, assuming the shape of mummies, if left to themselves. And I wondered if every cave possessed a similar altar, and if the whole island had simply been a place of sacrifice and death for some prehistoric race living in other islands round about, like those on the horizon we could still see; or perhaps long ages ago engulfed in some great cataclysm of nature and sunk beneath the ocean these thousands of years and then raised again.

Turning away from the altar to the right we found the way clear, and with a sigh of relief I drew Mistress Lucy reluctantly on. She clung to me and was so frightened that I finally slipped my arm about her waist, whereat she made no objection. She has confessed since that she was indeed greatly pleased and that it was a comfort to her to feel the strength and power of my grasp.

Holding the lantern before me, I cautiously proceeded further into the cave toward the inner wall. The cave wall apparently opened out into rooms. I did not dare go any distance from the main entrance for fear that I should lose my way, so I stopped undecided what to do; which opening to enter, that is.

"Oh, let us go back," begged my mistress, "there is no treasure here, I am sure."

"Nay," I answered, "with your permission, Mistress Wilberforce, I intend to explore further into the matter. Let us see." I held the lantern high above my head as I spoke. There above the entrance I saw a rude Latin cross! "Look," I continued, "someone has been here, 'tis the sign of the cross!"

"Yes," she said, her hopes reviving and her spirits returning a little at the unwonted sight of that sacred symbol of our faith in this place of idolatry and superstition, "don't you remember on the map marking the position of the cave there was a little cross?"

"So there was," I exclaimed, "although the reading did not mention it."

"No, but it is there, nevertheless."

I stooped down—the entrance was scarcely three feet high but quite broad—and made to go through.

"Wait!" She seized me in great alarm. "You cannot go in there and leave me here," she cried.

"I promise you that I will not stir three feet from the entrance, if you will suffer me that far," I answered.

"I must come, too, then," she urged.

"I will see what is there first, and if it is safe you shall come with me immediately," I answered, giving her no time for further objection.

As I spoke, I crawled through and found myself in another smaller chamber. There being no visible danger, I stretched out my hand to her and brought her through after me. From some distant crevice the air came to us, we could feel it blow upon us, and it was sweet. Also I could hear water bubbling over rocks in the distance. It was a little damp in the cave, perhaps because of that. There was little light, however, save that cast by the lantern. I could not see the further wall.

We did not need to go further into the cave, for there before us, clearly enough revealed by the dim radiance of the lamp, lay a number of large wooden boxes or chests, moldy and ancient. The boxes had once been iron strapped, but we found the iron had rusted and the wood had rotted. I stepped over to one of them, lifted the lid which crumbled at my touch, and there was the treasure—ingots of gold and silver! Thousands of pounds lay to our hands! The old buccaneer had told the truth. The story of the parchment was not a romance, the plunder of the ancient galleon was there.

I have read, as you all have, the great romance of Daniel DeFoe, and the uselessness of this mass of gold and silver of which the Spaniards had robbed the natives, making them toil to death in the mines, for which Sir Philip Wilberforce's men had fought and died, for which the men on *The Rose of Devon* had committed murder, and which, had we been able to dispose of it, would have bought anything the world had to offer, came home to me, as in similar circumstances Robinson Crusoe had the same thought. For my part I would gladly have exchanged it all for a stout boat and a clear passage through the reef with a chance for freedom.

"Well, your great-great-great-grandfather, for how many generations back I know not, was right," I said at last. "The treasure is here and we have found it. It is yours."

"Yes," she said, to whom the same thought had come, "but now that we have found it of what value or use is it?"

"None," I admitted, "that I can see that is, but there is a certain satisfaction in having found it, and in knowing that you can own it even if you cannot take it away. I am glad that events have proved that we came on no fool's errand."

"And what may be its value, think you?"

"It would make good ballast for a ship," I answered lightly.

"But if we could take it hence to England?"

"Millions, I can only guess."

"I will give you one-half of it for your share," she said, laughing softly.

"I want none of it," I returned seriously enough.

What possessed her to do it, I know not, and she has since confessed she knows not either. We stood there, looking down upon the useless heap of treasure, when she turned to me on a sudden.

"Now that you have seen it, are you still of the same mind," she asked mischievously, "that you would give up your portion of the treasure—for me?"

The Island of the Stairs

"Great God!" I exclaimed, moved beyond measure by her imprudent remark, and thrown off my balance by her—dare I say coquetry? "I would give up the world itself for you. Don't you know it?"

And I made a step toward her, but she put up her hand.

"Hush! stay! Master Hampdon," she cried affrighted at the consequences of her pleasantry, "remember—"

"I shall never forget," I said grimly. "This treasure removes you further away from me than ever."

"What mean you?"

"When you get back to England and take your place once more among your friends in that society to which your birth entitles you and which this wealth will enable you to sustain—"

"And who is to take me back to England?"

"I."

"How?"

"I know not, but I shall do it."

"And with the treasure?"

"With the treasure, too, at least a sufficiency of it for all your needs."

"And when you have done this amazing thing for me, you expect to disappear from my life, Master Hampdon?"

"Aye, if need be."

She laughed, and I did not understand the meaning of that laugh, either.

"Is it not idle for us to speculate upon treasures which we cannot carry hence, and which in our present situation are not so useful to us as the little pieces of flint and steel with the tinder in the pocket of your coat?" she asked, smiling.

"You are right," I answered, smiling in turn, although what it cost me to smile in the face of the picture of the future that came to me, you cannot imagine. "But let us search and see if there be anything else. Your ancestor spoke of jewels."

The Island of the Stairs

"Yes," she said, "there should be a smaller casket, let us look further."

There were perhaps a dozen large boxes. I opened them all. Some were quite empty, with little piles of dust in them, and a few shreds of color here and there which indicated silk had been packed in them. There were also broken barrels around which still clung a faint odor of spices. There were piles of rotted débris further on, and as I stirred one of them with my sheath sword I struck something more solid. I brushed aside what seemed to be the decayed remains of cordage and wood and finally came upon a smaller casket bound, strapped, hinged, and cornered with some kind of metal which I afterward found to be silver—iron would have rusted long since. The casket was about a foot long by six inches wide and six inches deep. The metal which completely covered it was curiously chased. The casket was locked. I crumbled the wood in my hands, but could not open the lock. The edge of my axe, however, proved a potent key and at last I forced it apart. As I did so out fell a little heap of what I judged to be precious stones. There were green, red, blue, and white ones, among them many pearls sadly discolored and valueless. The stones glistened with an almost living energy. My mistress was more familiar with these things than I, and I presented a handful to her.

"Why, they are precious stones!" she cried, in an awe-struck whisper. "Look," she held up a diamond as big as her thumb nail; it sparkled like a sun in the candlelight. "And there is an emerald," she cried, picking up one of the green stones, "this blue one is a sapphire, this a ruby. Why," she exclaimed, "here is a fortune alone. These jewels must be of fabulous value. The gold and silver we might leave behind, but these we can carry with us."

In my heart I was sorry we had found them, yet I had the grace immediately to say,

"I am glad for that. We must gather them up, but where shall we put them?"

"In the pockets of your coat for the present," she answered.

Now there were not so many of them, perhaps three or four handfuls, not nearly enough to fill the casket. I figured that it had been a jewel box with little trays or drawers, and that the stones had been wrapped separately but had all fallen together when the partitions rotted away. I easily found room for them in the capacious side pockets of my coat and then we turned back to the outer room. Passing by the hideous altar we gained the open day again. It was now late in the afternoon, we found to our surprise. And yet how sweet it was, that outer air, after those caves of death and treasure!

We had spent hours over the search, and we had just time to retrace our steps and get back to the boat on the beach and partake of our evening meal when night fell. As we sat by the fire that night, I made two little bags out of a piece of canvas taken from a bread bag, and we put the jewels into them, dividing them into equal parts. One bag she wore constantly thereafter on her person, and I the other.

My mistress was at first anxious to stow them away in some crack or cranny of the rock, but I said, I scarcely knew why, that it would be better to keep them always with us, and so we did. She insisted that the rough and ready division we had made was permanent, that the bag I carried belonged to me and the bag she carried belonged to her. But I refused to have it so in spite of her argument and there we left it.

CHAPTER XV
WHEREIN THE SERPENT ENTERS THE EDEN

DURING the next two or three days we leisurely explored the island. There was much in it of interest, of course, but nothing else which merits any particular description or has any bearing on this story. We did not again visit the central hill, nor did we enter any other cave. We did not even go near the treasure cave again, on the contrary we kept to the open. There were charming groves within the walls, but we could not bear to be shut up within the great cup. It seemed not unlike a prison to us. Outside we could at least see the vast expanse of the restless ocean. We chose to live near the sea on the beach which was high above all tides and which was far removed from the charnel spots which made a mockery of the sylvan groves within the walls. The island was well provided with tropical fruits, many being good for food, as I knew. We caught fish in the lagoon and turtle on the sand. We could make a fire and cook our food. There was salt in plenty. My tailoring and cobbling stood the test. We lacked nothing to make us comfortable, even happy, except the means of escape. My comrade was never in better health in her life. Roses bloomed in her cheeks again and I—I was more than contented in her society.

We spent our days in trying to devise some means of getting across the reef and back home again, that is when I was not idly lying at the feet or following the footsteps of the woman I loved. I didn't want to get away so far as I was concerned. I didn't care whether we ever got away. I had wit enough not to let her see, not to let her suspect that for a moment, however—at least I made the endeavor—and I tried to convince her by my actions at least that my kissing her on the ship had been but a momentary madness, but I learned later that I failed lamentably. She says now that a baby could see that I was dying for her, and I suppose it is true, but at least I didn't say anything. After that outbreak in the cave I kept silence.

As I look back upon those days I scarcely think she treated me kindly, and yet I know not. I was at once happy and miserable—very happy in her presence, very miserable in the thought that I was and could be nothing to her. She played upon me as if I had been a pipe, she led me on and she repelled me, she drew me and she drove me. I had wit, however, to see that she was enjoying it, even if I did not; and I was in some measure content that she should be glad. It was a fool's paradise in which we lived. We had no care, nothing could touch us, nothing could hurt us—at least so we fancied. We had water in plenty and enough to eat of pleasant variety, fruit, fish fresh caught from the lagoon, the meat and eggs of the turtle, relieved by the edibles we had brought from the ship, of which we still had some small store left. The air was soft and balmy, the birds sang, the flowers bloomed. We were young, I loved blindly, passionately; she, as I know now though I never suspected it then, with her beautiful eyes open—that is if eyes that love are ever open. Eden, Eden! Ah it was there!

We made frequent trips up the stairs and into the cup of the island, we traversed as much of the wall as possible, although that was but little because the sharp, jagged edges when we left the path would have cut our feet to pieces. We fished, we launched the boat on the lagoon and rowed clear around the island. I left her sometimes that she might refresh herself in dips within the cool water, while I did the same further away and out of sight. Like Adam and Eve we lived in that Garden and dallied with the forbidden fruit even if we did not eat it. Aye, and the serpent came, as of old, into that soft Pacific Paradise.

Late one afternoon we stood at the head of the stairs looking seaward. We had come from a long ramble throughout the cup of the island and as we stood on the top our gaze as usual instinctively turned toward the sea, perhaps seeking for the sail of some rescuing ship. The water was black with great formidable looking war canoes!

We could not believe our eyes at first. We stared at the water in amazement, motionless, awe-struck, appalled. This time it was I who came to my senses first.

"Great God!" I cried, "look yonder."

"I see, I see," she cried, in turn. "Who can they be?"

"Dwellers from the other islands to the westward," I answered.

They could not see us yet fortunately but, after all, that mattered little save as a temporary respite. Strangely enough, my lady did not seem to be nearly so disturbed as I.

"The reef will protect us again," she said at last, looking at me confidently.

"Not for a moment," I answered, "they will ride that reef in those light canoes more easily than we did."

"And you think—" she instantly began.

"Our lives are in God's hands. If I know anything these will be ferocious, bloodthirsty savages. See, they are armed."

I pointed to one tall brown man who stood up in the bow of the nearest canoe, flourishing a broad-bladed spear.

"We must hide," she said.

"But where? They will search the whole island as soon as they discover our boat and other belongings and realize that some strangers are here. Where can we find concealment?"

"In the treasure cave, of course," she answered promptly.

And indeed that was the most likely spot. We had brought but little with us that afternoon. I had thrust a brace of pistols in my belt and she herself, by my advice, always carried her two smaller ones, and I had my sword and axe, but everything else was with the boat on the beach under the cliff. For a moment I thought of running down there and getting some of our things, but as I half turned to descend the stairs, she detained me, divining my purpose.

"No, no," she urged, clasping my arm with both hands, "we must make shift with what we have. You could not go and come in time. Perhaps they may not discover us, they may not understand the boat if they are only savages. We can hide safely until they depart, it may be. Come, let us go."

There was sense in her remarks. It might be that after performing some awful worship these most unwelcome visitors would return as they came. And by keeping closely hid we might escape an encounter with them. As ever in the emergency she gave the better counsel. Nevertheless, I deplored more than I can say that I could not get to the arms and other things under the cliff on the beach near the boat. They would certainly find everything as soon as they crossed the reef and landed, although what it would tell them and what they would do only time would determine. But there was no help for that now. We had to make the best of a bad situation.

We turned and ran back down the path across the wall. I had forethought to gather a number of cocoanuts and some other fruit as we passed. I filled my own pockets and then she made a bag out of her tunic and carried the rest. Presently I reflected that we had no need for such haste. There would be plenty of time for us to reach the cave and conceal ourselves long before they landed, so we progressed more slowly. It was almost dusk when we reached our shelter. I had uprooted a small tree just before we started to climb the pile of stones which I used as a lever to push down the heap in every direction as we climbed so that it would be impossible for anyone else to enter the cave without piling up the stones again. We passed by the stone altar and its skeletons, crept into the inner room, flung ourselves panting upon the sand and there we waited.

In that secret and secluded shelter I thought that we were safe for the time being. Especially was I sure that they would make no effort to find us at night, as the place had anciently been some sort of a shrine and was probably held sacred still. And in the morning I did not think that they would chance upon that particular cave out of the many in the coral walls without a long search, unless they had proposed coming just there for other reasons than we attributed to them. Even if they did stumble upon our hiding place early in the hunt, which I felt sure would be made for us as soon as they discovered evidences of our presence on the island in the shape of the dinghy, or at least at daybreak, it would take them some time to rebuild the pyramid of rock against the wall again; and when they did enter the outer room they would find it a matter of extreme difficulty to get into the inner chamber so long as I was there. Unfortunately, we had brought no powder and ball with us. We had no means of reloading our firearms, once they had been discharged. I resolved to reserve the four pistols we had for the last emergency.

For other weapons I had my axe and sword, to say nothing of the loose stones and even of the human skulls about the altar.

I have said, I think, that the inner cave was slightly damp. The dampness rose from a spring of water which bubbled away in some dark corner which we had not cared to explore. We had what provisions we had brought with us left over from our luncheon, which I had luckily preserved instead of throwing them away, and an armful of cocoanuts and other fruit. These, however, would last us but a short while. If they could not come at us by force, they could easily starve us out. Also they could, without too much trouble or danger, make themselves masters of the outer cave. Indeed, I scarcely thought it would be wise for me to attempt to prevent that, and in that case they could wall up the entrance and leave us there.

It did not occur to us for a single moment that they had any knowledge of the treasure, and that they could be after that. Not for even the thousandth part of a second did I dream the savages were led by Pimball, Glibby, and most of the other seamen of *The Rose of Devon*. I did not know then, although I have since heard the whole story from the survivors, that *The Rose of Devon* had gone ashore in the terrific storm I have described, there had been a battle with the savages who sought to plunder the ship, but which was prevented at frightful loss to the islanders who were unable to contend successfully against the firearms with which the ship was so abundantly provided. A means of communication between the ship and the shore had been found subsequently, through one of the seamen who had sailed the South Seas. The savages had been told of the treasure, of which indeed they had some dim traditions from days gone by; they also held the cave as one of their most sacred spots, scarcely less sacred than the great altar on the hillock in the center of the island, for what reason I cannot tell.

By some persuasion, I know not what, Pimball and Glibby had won them over. Together they had organized an expedition to come and seize us and take the treasure. *The Rose of Devon* was not badly damaged, she had been floated and found to be still seaworthy. The savages naturally cared little or nothing for the gold or silver, and I divined later that Pimball had promised to turn us over to them for such purposes as the reader can well imagine. After tortures, we would inevitably be killed and eaten.

I did not figure this out then, of course. If I had guessed it, I believe I should have been so blindly furious that I should have sallied out and attacked them at the giant stairs. Indeed, that would have been no bad place for defense if the stairway had been but a little narrower. Had I been alone perhaps I should have defied them there, but I had my lady to look to and I dared take no chances. I could not force the fighting.

We sat silent in the cave for a long time. I had not lighted the ship's lantern we had left there at our last visit, having no use for it elsewhere on the island, since we went to bed at dark and rose at dawn, for some of the light of the dying day filtered through from the outside cave. There was nothing that we needed light for anyway. We sat close together on the remains of one of the chests to protect us from the damp sand. I always carried with me a flask of spirits. Not that I am a drinking man, I left and still leave that practice to the gallants of the day, but I have found it useful in some dire emergency, and now as Mistress Lucy shivered in the chill, damp air, I heartened her and strengthened her with a dram.

As it was summer and not far from the line, I had not brought the boat cloak with us. I had not even worn my sailor's jacket, but my mutilated leather waistcoat was heavy and warm and I was thankful that I had it. The pieces which I had cut from it for the soles of her little shoes had not spoiled it for wear either, since I had been careful in their selection. I took it off and despite her protestations slipped it on her. In girth it was big enough to encircle her twice, which was all the better for her comfort. I drew it around to cover her breast with a double fold and with a length of line I had in my pocket I made it fast. We sat close together and talked in low whispers and I thrilled at the contact of her sweet presence in spite of our peril.

How long we talked or how long we waited I have no means of telling. It grew dark in the cave very early and when I ventured into the outside room after what seemed an interminable wait, I found night had fallen. I felt pretty sure that we need apprehend no attack that night and yet it was necessary to keep watch, so I proposed that one of us should sleep while the other listened. Naturally she was the first to take rest. It was too damp and cold to lie down on the sand, so I wedged myself against one of the least rotted of the chests whose shape had been kept intact by the pile of gold and silver bars it had contained, and somewhat hesitatingly offered her the shelter of my arm.

"Madam," I said, with all the formality I could muster, "you must have sleep. You cannot lie upon this damp sand, it is bad enough to sit upon it; but upon my shoulder and within the support of my arm you shall have rest."

"I trust you," she replied, coming closer to me, "and if I am to sleep I know that I shall be safe within your arms."

"As my sister, had I one, or as my mother, were she alive and here, will I support you," said I, which was, I must admit, untrue, for I had a great to-do to keep my arm from trembling, and I felt sure she would hear my heart throbbing madly when she nestled close to me, her head upon my shoulder. And she has since admitted that she did feel the tremor and hear the throb, whereat she was most glad. But I knew nothing of that then, nor for a long time after.

Before she closed her eyes, however, she made her evening prayer for herself and for me, and then she made me promise that I would awaken her when I judged it to be midnight, and upon my promise she nestled down and went to sleep, her head upon my shoulder. Surely never had man a more precious charge than I that night!

I sat there motionless, my bared sword at my side, listening. I could hear nothing, no sound except her soft breathing and once in a while the sough of the night wind through the trees outside, which penetrated faintly into the cave, and at more infrequent intervals the cry of some night bird came to me, but there was no sound of humanity. How long I sat there, I know not. It was my purpose to keep awake the night through, and I think I must have kept awake the greater part thereof, but toward morning my head dropped back on the pile of ingots and I fell asleep. Yet I did not relax my clasp upon the sleeping figure lying upon my breast. It was she who awakened when the dim light began to sift through the narrow opening into the little cave where we sat.

CHAPTER XVI
IN WHICH WE ARE BELEAGUERED IN THE CAVE

"MASTER HAMPTON," she said, bending over me, having arisen without disturbing me, "it is morning."

I sprang to my feet instantly, as she shook me gently, and grasped my sword as I did so, whereat she laughed.

"Why did you not awaken me?" she asked reprovingly.

"I don't know, I must have—" I began in great confusion.

"You must have gone to sleep yourself," she laughed again, and I marveled, but thankfully, to see her so cheerful.

"I am ashamed," I replied, "that I should have failed in my duty to keep good watch. I didn't awaken you when I might because you needed sleep yourself, and then like a great animal I went to sleep myself."

"I am glad," she said, smiling at me, and I could just see her lovely face faintly in the dark twilight of the cave, "that you did since nothing happened."

"It is just as well then," I said, smiling in turn, "we have both slept soundly and well. I feel greatly refreshed."

"And I."

"Thank God," I said fervently.

"What is to be done now?" she asked.

"First breakfast."

I broke open a cocoanut with my axe, I had become expert at it, and we had food and drink in plenty, and for variety some of the hard bread which still remained and other fruit. I lighted the lantern for a moment and went toward the sound of the falling water. The cocoanut shell made an excellent cup and I brought her enough clear, cool, sweet water to lave her face and hands. Save for the stiffness of the constrained position and some slight pain caused by the damp we were both fit for any adventure. Well, we should have need of all our strength doubtless. When we finished our meal and our refreshing ablutions, she looked at me inquiringly.

"Well, what next?"

"The next thing," said I, "is to see what is toward."

"You won't leave the cave," she said, catching me by the shoulder.

"I should find it difficult were I so minded," I answered, smiling and thrilling to her touch again as always. Indeed, I have never got used to it even after all these years. As I look back on the scenes of the past now I do not think I have ever had happier moments in my life than those in which she clung to me and was dependent upon me.

"Why not?" she asked.

"You forget that we broke down the way last night."

"But you are a sailor, you might make shift."

"Yes, but not you," I answered.

"Without me?"

"Without you I go nowhere."

She looked at me with shining eyes.

"Come," said I, "let us go into the outer room. We may find out something."

I had wound my watch in the dark and looked at it now as we came into the light. It was three bells in the morning watch, or about half after nine. We went past the altar with its grim bony circle of attendants, and stared through the entrance. There was an open space at the foot of the cliff forty or fifty yards wide perhaps before the jungle began. After looking some time and seeing nothing I foolishly—and yet it would have made no difference in the end—stepped out upon the shelf which made a sort of platform in front of the cave and Mistress Lucy fearlessly came with me.

We had scarcely appeared in view when to our astounded surprise we heard the report of a firearm and a heavy bullet struck the coral wall just over our heads. I had just time to mark the spot whence it came, by the betraying smoke, as I leaped back into the shelter

The Island of the Stairs

carrying my precious charge before me. I was puzzled beyond measure. I was certain that the savages in these parts of the South Seas knew nothing about firearms and I could not account for it. The shower of arrows and spears that now came through the opening and fell harmlessly on the sand I could easily account for, but not that shot. What could it mean? I felt that I could hold my own against savages without difficulty, but if there were European enemies there the case was different.

"That," said I solemnly, "was a narrow escape."

"Do these islanders have firearms?" she asked, the same thought in her mind.

"I never heard of it," I replied. "I cannot account for it."

"I can, though," she said; "just before the discharge of that gun I caught sight of a man in clothes such as you wear. Is it possible that it could be one from *The Rose of Devon*?"

I nodded my head, a light at once breaking upon me.

"It is quite likely," I answered, "now it is certain."

At this moment our further conversation was interrupted by a hail. To our great amazement we heard in that lonely island my own name called! That hail could only come from a survivor of the ship. It confirmed our surmises about the shot.

"Master Hampdon," the cry came to us, "will you respect a flag of truce? If so, show yourself at the opening and I shall do the same."

"Don't go," cried my little mistress, hearing all, "they are utterly without honor, and—"

"I think it will be best for me to appear," I said. "Stand clear so that if any treacherous movement be made I shall have space to leap backward, and meanwhile look to your weapons."

I examined my own pistols and then calling out loudly that I would faithfully observe the flag of truce, I stepped out into the open. There below me on the edge of the glade, convenient to a tree behind which he could leap, for the rascal trusted me apparently as little as I trusted him, stood the wretch, Pimball. Back of him beneath the trees

The Island of the Stairs

I distinguished Glibby and a number of the crew, nearly all of them, I should judge, and back of these were massed the savages. Pimball had a white neckcloth tied to the muzzle of his gun.

"Good morning, Master Hampdon," he began suavely.

To that salutation I made no reply. I did not deign even to pass the time of day with such a man as he.

"Say what you have to say and be quick about it," I said haughtily, but he looked past me and took off his hat with a profound sweep.

"Good morning, Mistress Wilberforce," he cried.

I turned in a hurry and found that she had stepped out by my side, completely disobeying my positive direction. The two of us presented a fair mark for any weapon; one might escape, but hardly two if Pimball's men opened fire.

"Get back!" I cried harshly in mingled amazement and dismay.

"I stay where you are," she answered firmly. "See, I, too, am armed," her little hand lifted her own pistol.

"I can talk with the two of you jest as well as with one, or even better," interposed Pimball smoothly, "an' the lady won't need her pistol."

"Talk on and be brief," I returned, seeing there was no use in arguing with my little mistress who always did have her own way in the end.

Yet I did take the precaution to interpose my bulk between the man on the ground and my lady who strove to move around me, but I stubbornly held my position and compelled her to keep in the background where she was in less danger.

"You've found the treasure," he began, "there ain't no use denyin' it; we've l'arnt from our savage friends that the stuff is there. In years gone by they sacrificed here an' on the cone yonder, but for generations the island has been taboo. The comin' of the white man has broke the ban an' we're here to take the treasure away with us."

"Indeed!" said I sarcastically, whereat he turned pale with anger but still mastered himself.

The Island of the Stairs

"She had stepped out by my side."

"We offer you," he continued, "safety. We can't take you with us, but we'll leave you here on the island arter we have fetched away the treasure."

"Thank you," I returned, "you are vastly kind."

He bit his lip at that and then his eyes turned from me to my companion.

"If you are willin' to give up the woman," he said suddenly, revealing his real villainy, "I'll enroll you with our followin' an' we'll all git away together on *The Rose of Devon*."

"What of the ship?" I asked.

It was a hard thing to control my temper, but I wanted the information and until I got it I must command myself.

"She was badly damaged when she took ground on the sand durin' the storm but not entirely wrecked, an' is still seaworthy. We've patched her up, too. We can git away in her an' you can navigate her, or we can do without you, for that matter, an' make shift to git her back to the South American coast at least."

"So you offer me free passage and my share of the treasure if I will give up Mistress Wilberforce, do you?"

"That's just it," answered Pimball. "Eh, mates?" whereat a deep chorus of approval came from Glibby and the men.

"And this is my answer," I said furiously, leveling my pistol at him. "Get back, you villain, or you will have looked your last on life."

"But the flag of truce," he cried, dropping his weapon in surprise.

"It is not meant to cover such propositions as yours. As for the treasure, you shall have it when you can get it."

As I spoke he sprang behind the tree and motioned to his men to fire, but I was too quick for him, and we were safely behind the walls of the cave when the sound of the reports came to us. I had carried my mistress there before me in my unceremonious backward rush.

"It was bravely said," began my lady, "but if I were not here, you—"

I laughed.

"You are here and if you were not they would murder me like a sheep when they had got out of me all they wanted."

"Yes," said she, "I suppose so. Now what is to be done?"

"The next move," said I, "is with them."

"Shall we go further back into the cave?"

"No, we will stay here for the moment," I replied.

We were not long left in suspense for I could hear them breaking through the woods and rushing toward the entrance. Missiles in the way of weapons there were none in the cave, but I picked up a skull that lay on the floor and hurled it out of the opening into the unseen crowd below on a venture. A shriek told me that I had hit someone, but I saw at once that the game was one I could not play longer, for a rain of missiles, stones, arrows, what not, fell in the entrance.

These villainous white men had some skill at warfare, it seemed. They had posted covering parties to protect the workmen who had been detailed to repair and make possible the approach. I stepped cautiously toward the entrance and peered down. I could see them working hard, piling up the stones to enable them to get at us, while back of them others stood with drawn bows and presented weapons.

I did not come off unscathed, for as I sprang back after having thrown another skull and taken my look, an arrow hit me in the fleshy part of my arm. My mistress noticed it instantly. The stone head had broken off and it was the work of an instant to draw out the slender wood shaft. It was not at all a bad wound but it was quite painful. The next thing she did amazed me beyond measure, for before I could prevent it my mistress had put her lips to the wound.

"What mean you?" I cried when I could recover myself.

"It might have been poisoned," she said quietly, looking at me with luminous eyes, "and I cannot have you die!"

CHAPTER XVII
HOW WE FIGHT FOR LIFE IN THE CAVERN OF THE TREASURE

I WAS amazed, astounded even, at her hardihood in sucking any possible poison out of that wound in my arm at so great a risk to her own life, if the weapon had been envenomed. And I was most profoundly touched, too. But as I had had my lesson on the ship I presumed no further; I viewed it as done out of common humanity and to preserve a life useful to her—nothing more. I dared not put any other construction upon her noble action, even in thought. Meanwhile in my turn, I took such hasty precautions for her safety as I could while I thanked her. I bade her rinse out her mouth thoroughly with a mixture of the cold water and the strong spirit of which I still had my flask nearly full.

By this time we had withdrawn to the back of the outer cave. Indeed, that was the only safe place for us, for a constant succession of weapons was being thrown through the opening. We needed no further warning to keep us out of reach. Master Pimball was showing himself something of a general, too. He was keeping us away from the entrance and with the great host of men at his command he was building up the broken-down heap of stones which would presently enable them to come at us in force. At least that was what I guessed from what I had seen and what I now heard.

While my little mistress busied herself with tying up my wounded arm with strips torn from the sleeve of my shirt which I had offered for the purpose—she had wanted to make bandages out of her underwear but I stayed her—I considered what was to be done. I had four loaded pistols and therefore four lives in my hand. No man could show his head in that entrance without receiving a shot. After that I could account for a few more, perhaps, with sword, axe, or naked fist, but in the end they would inevitably master me. Unfortunately, the entrance was broad enough for four or more to enter abreast easily.

Should I open the battle there or retreat into the inner cave and wait, was the question that had to be decided. Perhaps the latter would be the safer plan but I had a strange unwillingness to adopt it, for once within I feared we should never get out alive except as prisoners, so long as they held the outer cave and I could never dislodge them from it. There was not much more chance of getting out alive from the outer cave, for that matter, but still it seemed so. We could at least see the sky and the sunlight. Should we stay there or go further into the wall?

I decided upon the former course. I explained to my mistress that I would keep the outer cave as long as I could, begging her to retreat to the inner chamber. She demurred at first, but when I spoke to her peremptorily at last—God forgive me—she acceded to my request humbly enough. Indeed, she saw that in this matter I could not be denied and also perhaps that I had right and prudence on my side. Her presence would only have embarrassed me in my fighting although I could quite understand that she wanted to fight, too. It was in her blood and she has since confessed that she never expected that we would come through the conflict alive and she would fain have died by my side. But that was not to be, and so, for the once she obeyed me.

I thrust the best pistol into her hand and told her to reserve it for herself in case her capture was inevitable, but not to pull the trigger until the last moment. And I promised her faithfully that I would not foolishly or uselessly jeopard myself but that after I had made what fight I could, I would join her if it were in any way possible.

Even then she hung in the wind awhile, seeming loath to go when all had been said between us. Finally she approached me, laid her hand on my arm and looked up at me. Seeing that she had previously decided to go and said so, I wondered what was coming now.

"Master Hampdon," she said softly, "here we be a lone man and woman among these savages and murderers with but little chance for our lives, I take it. I am sorry that I struck you on the ship—and—you may—kiss—me—good-by."

With that she proffered me her lips. I could face a thousand savages, a hundred Pimballs, without a quiver of the nerves, but at these unexpected words and that wonderful condescension, my knees fairly smote together before this small woman. I stood staring down at her.

"You were once over eager to take from me by force what I now offer you willingly," she said, half turning away in a certain—shall I say disappointment?

With that I caught her to me and once again I drank the sweetness of her lips. We were bound to die and I kissed her as a man does when he loves a woman. I forgot the savages outside, the stones, the spears, the arrows streaming through the entrance, the yells and curses that came to us. I held her in my arms and without resistance. I could have held her there forever, quite willing to die in such sweet embrace. She pushed me away from her at last and I could swear that my kisses had been returned, and then with a whispered blessing she dropped to her knees and crawled within the adjoining cave.

I could have fought the world, thereafter, for her kisses intoxicated me like wine. Yet even then I did not delude myself. I felt that on her part at least, it was a farewell kiss such as two true devoted comrades might give to each other in the face of death. I said to myself that to her the pressure of my lips had only been as the salute of an ancient gladiator about to die was to the Cæsar who watched the struggle. To me—well I blessed her even for that crowning mercy.

With a pistol in each hand and the third upon a rock close at hand I waited. I had not long to wait. There was a sudden fiercer rain of arrows and spears, some of which struck at my feet or by my side. I gathered up a sheaf of them and laid them at hand beside the pistol on the rock.

The next instant two tremendous savages and a white man appeared in the entrance. The shot was easy, the target fine. I couldn't miss. The first bullet went into the brain of Master Glibby, the next tore off the head of the leading chief. Reserving the third pistol, I seized a spear and drove it through the throat of the other savage. I shouted with triumph, and Mistress Lucy has since confessed to me that, kneeling down and peering through the opening, contrary to my explicit order which was for her to seek safe cover, she saw all and that my call of victory was the sweetest sound she had ever heard.

The Island of the Stairs

I thought we had done, but they were an indomitable lot, those South Sea islanders, and they were well urged. Four others took their places at once, spears in hands, which they threw at me. I dodged them with some difficulty and let fly the third pistol. They came crowding this time and the bullet from the heavy weapon accounted for two others, but the survivors had gained a footing, and the shelf behind them was suddenly filled with lifting heads and climbing men.

I clubbed my weapons and hurled them one after another fair and square into the mass. One man went down with a broken skull. The rush was checked, they gave back a little. I cast spears and arrows at them but now the shield men had come up and they caught the missiles on their shields. The front rank wavered and perhaps if they had been unsupported, they might have been driven below, but the crowd behind would not let them retire. Slowly they began to move toward me.

I doubt not I was a terrible figure, for I had whipped out my cutlass by this time and stood at bay. I had forgotten for the moment all else but the lust of the conflict and in another second I had flung myself upon them in a fury. It was my mistress who recalled me to myself.

"Save yourself," she shrieked, "they are upon you. Come hither."

With that I dropped down and made a spring for the opening. I had waited too long. The leading man would have pinned me to the earth with his spear. The entrance was wide fortunately, and Mistress Lucy would see through the part I did not block with my huge bulk. Again disregarding entirely my instructions, she fired the last pistol at that nearest man. He went down like a ninepin, both legs broken, which gave me time to gain the inner chamber and stand upright. I was bleeding for I had been cut here and there, but was otherwise all right.

"That shot saved my life," I cried panting, "you should have kept it for yourself."

"I can find means to die," she answered, "if by naught else, by your sword blade."

"Good," I exclaimed, proud of her prowess and her resolution.

They gave us no time for further speech for urged by what promises of reward, what passionate hatred, what bestial desire, I know not, they came on. The narrow entrance was suddenly black with the islanders who thrust their spears at us. Fortunately my mistress had moved aside and was out of range, but I was perilously near being cut down. Mistress Lucy had the sword which I had thrust into her hand, and I the great axe which I had cast into the inner cave ahead of me.

Those outside were even less able to see than we and perhaps they thought we had withdrawn, or been driven back, for they crept forward with assurance.

While I had lived in the gardener's lodge at Wilberforce Castle, I had got to be quite an axe-man. I brought down the heavy weapon on the first head, striking with just enough force to kill and yet leave me able to recover myself without delay, and when three heads had been knocked that way in rapid succession with no more damage to me than a trifling spear cut on the ankle, the battle stopped for a moment. I laughed.

"Come on, you dogs!" I shouted, "I can play at that game until you are more tired of it than I."

I spoke without thought, however, for those outside the opening drew back the bodies by their legs and thus cleared the entrance. I judged that the outer cave, which was large and spacious, was now filled with men. They were shouting and gesticulating in great excitement. But none made any effort to enter. Finally, I heard a human voice speaking English. It was Pimball.

"Master Hampdon?" he cried.

"Speak not to me, murdering villain," I answered.

"Now this is madness," he shouted. "You are trapped like rats; we have only to wall up the entrance or build a fire in front of it an' you will both die."

"It is a thousand times better to die so," I answered shortly, "than to live with craven men like you."

"You are a fool," he exclaimed.

He dropped down on his knees as he spoke and I could see his face in the opening but too far away for me to swing my axe. If it were my last effort I was determined that I would get him, and so I waited.

"Don't lose the sword," I cried to my lady across the chamber where her white face stared at me out of the dimness.

"I shall not," she answered undauntedly.

Then I lifted the axe and waited for Master Pimball and his men to come on, but he had a better plan. Bullets and powder they had in plenty and he knew from the fact that I had thrown my pistols at them that I had none left. With a deafening roar a storm of bullets from a dozen weapons swept the cave. I leaped back. I had to, or I should have been shot where I stood. Of the way thus opened they took instant advantage and under cover of a second volley they sought to enter. Well, it was all up, all I could do was to leap upon them as they rose and —

But that moment the solid rock beneath my feet began to sway. It was as if I had been instantly translated to the deck of a tossing ship. I stood rooted to the spot trying to maintain a balance. Pimball had lifted himself upon one knee and was almost clear of the entrance, but he too stopped, appalled. A sickening feeling of apprehension that all the savages on earth would not have inspired came over me. My mistress screamed faintly. The natives outside broke into terror stricken shouts and cries, an oath burst from the lips of the leader of the mutineers.

The next moment, with a crash like a thousand thunder peals the earth was rent in twain.

The earthquake shook that rocky island like a baby's cradle. A great mass of rock over the entrance fell. With another roar like to the first the cliff was riven in every direction. The noise outside ceased. The men with Pimball were ground to death. Upon his legs lay fifty feet of broken rock. Darkness, total and absolute, succeeded the dim light. I remember realizing that the attack had failed and then something struck me. Down upon the wet, still quivering sand I fell and knew no more.

CHAPTER XVIII
IN WHICH WE PASS THROUGH DARKNESS TO LIGHT AND LIBERTY

WATER, icy cold, trickling upon me from some spring opened in the wall by the earthquake, presently brought me to myself. I lay for a moment listening. I could hear nothing at first, but in a little while a deep groan and then a faint whispered prayer came to me. I strove desperately to collect my senses and finally I realized where I was—the cave, the battle, the earthquake, the savages, Pimball, and the woman!

"Mistress Lucy!" I cried.

"Oh, thank God," her voice came through the darkness hysterically, "I thought you were killed."

"No," I answered, slowly rising to my knee and stretching my members to see if I had control of them, which fortunately I soon discovered I had, "I was stunned by falling rock, but otherwise I believe I am not much hurt. How is it with you?"

"I am well and unharmed."

"Now God be praised," I exclaimed fervently.

"For Christ's sake, water!" interposed a trembling, hoarse, anguished voice.

"Who speaks?" I asked.

"I, Pimball, I'm pinned to the ground, my back is broke, I'm dyin'."

"There should be a lantern here," I said. "I placed it—let me think, where did I place it?"

"It was just to the left of the opening," answered my little mistress.

I was turned around and giddy, but I managed to fix the direction of the entrance by Pimball's groans and by good fortune presently found the lantern. It would burn but a few hours, but we never needed a light as we did then, I decided. My flint and steel I carried ever in my pocket and to kindle a flickering flame was but the work of a moment. If I had not possessed it, I would have given years of

The Island of the Stairs

my life for even that feeble light which threw a faint illumination about the place.

There, opposite me where I had stationed her, by God's providence protected by a niche in the cave from the rain of rocks which had beaten me down, stood my mistress, safe and unharmed. I stepped toward her and with a low cry of thankfulness she fell into my arms. I soothed her for a moment and then turned to the other occupant of the chamber. The entrance was completely blocked up, the wall had settled down. Pimball's legs were broken and his back as well. It was impossible to release him, what lay upon him weighed tons and tons.

"You murdering hound," I cried, "you have brought this upon us," but he would only plead piteously for water, disregarding my bitter reproaches.

I was for killing him outright with my cutlass, which I picked up, but she would not have it so. She got a half cocoanut shell, filled it with water, and brought it to him. She bathed his brow and gave him some to drink. It gave him temporary relief but his minutes were numbered. His life was going out by seconds.

"God!" he cried, as his eyes caught the gleam of the gold and silver bars, "the treasure!" He stretched out his hand toward it, and then stopped. "I'm undone," he choked out with a fearful scream. "Mistress!"

"Yes?"

"Forgive—"

Indeed she forgave him, I make no doubt, but her forgiveness came too late, for his head dropped—he had been looking sideways—and his face buried itself in the wet sand.

"Is he dead?" she asked, awe-struck.

I nodded. No closer inspection was needed to establish the truth of that fact.

"He died with a prayer for forgiveness."

"And few men have ever had greater need for that forgiveness," said I, drawing her away.

"And we too shall die," she said shuddering. "We are buried here in the bowels of the earth, in this treasure lined prison."

"Well, we won't die without a struggle," I returned with more confidence than I felt.

"What mean you?"

"The earthquake which closed the mouth of the cave may have opened the other end."

"It is possible," she answered, "but not very likely."

"And besides, you remember the running stream on the other side of the cave, which we did not follow?"

"Yes."

"It must run somewhere."

"Well?"

"Where water runs men and women may find a way."

"At least it will do us no harm to try."

"Come then," said I, extending my hand to her and holding the lantern before me for pitfalls.

We went down the cave. To find the water was easy. Sure enough, it led away through a narrow rift, in what direction we could not tell, although its tendency was downward and I knew that it must come out upon the beach somewhere. It had not seemed to me, as I had examined it before the earthquake, that the rift was more than large enough to carry the water, but it might have been opened wider by the shock, and so we followed it. Although sometimes the walls closed over the watercourse, making low and narrow tunnels, we managed to force our way through them. I went in the advance, for I knew that what my body could pass would present no difficulty for her. We wandered in and out among the coral until it seemed to me that we had gone miles, although in reality it might have been but a few hundred yards.

At last we came to a place too low and too narrow for me, although I might have perhaps thrust her through.

"You see," she said, "this is the end."

"No, not yet," I answered, resolved never to give over the attempt while I could move hand or foot or draw a breath.

I still had the axe with me and the sword which I had thrust into my belt. The rock seemed soft and pliable. Lying down upon my back and covering my eyes with one hand, I struck at it overhead with the axe, which I grasped near the head, thus gradually enlarging the passage. The water flowing beneath me was deathly cold, the candle in the lantern was burning lower and lower, but I hung on. Never did I work so hard, so rapidly, so recklessly in my life as then. At last I loosened a huge piece of the rock which fell suddenly upon me. Had I not seen it coming and dropped the axe and stayed its progress with both upraised hands, it might have crushed me. As it was, it fell fairly upon my breast. I could not throw it aside, the way was too narrow. I held it off with my hands and forced my way through the opening, now barely enough to admit my passing, although what I should meet with or where I should bring up on the other side, I knew not. I had no idea how large the fallen rock was, for all its weight, but my mistress has told me that it was a monster stone, and that none but a giant could have carried it. I thrust hard and harder with my feet and presently my way was clear and I shoved myself through the opening. With one great final effort I rolled the rock aside and then lay on my back on the sand, breathless, exhausted.

She dragged herself through the passage I had thus made and over my body, and then knelt by my side, kissed me, murmuring words I did not dare to listen to lest I should go mad with joy. And indeed, I was so exhausted that I could scarcely credit that I had heard anything real. Presently, however, I staggered to my feet again. She had forgot the precious lantern, but I went back after it.

We were now in a more spacious cave; the stream fed by other brooks had become larger; the descent was much more rapid. The cliff wall was, I believe, narrower at the cave than anywhere else in the island. It was perhaps not more than half a mile wide. We stumbled rapidly down the long vaulted passage to the outer wall. As we approached it, I half feared that the rock might be solid and that the brook might plunge beneath it, but fortune did not do its worst for us yet. There was a rift in the wall around which the brook ran into a sort of tunnel or passageway, tall enough for me to stand upright and broad enough to enable us to walk side by side. A long distance away appeared to me a spot of dimness. Recklessly we clasped hands and ran.

Alas, when we reached the light, we found that the entrance was closed by a huge stone. It did not exactly fit the opening and light filtered around it. I stood panting, staring at it.

"Are we to be ended now," I cried, "after having come thus far? Stand clear, madam," I shouted, not giving her time to answer.

Then with all my strength I swung the axe and struck the rock fair and square and by good fortune upon some fissure, for it shivered and a crack started. Once again, this time with even more tremendous force, I swung and struck. The axe sank into the stone, the helve shivered in my hand. It was a right good blow, if I do say it myself, for the rock was now fairly split in two, the pieces falling to the right and left. Still, the two halves yet lay within the entrance, blocking it. We had not achieved a clear passage.

I was mad now, as mad as I had been in the outer cave fighting for her, or when I had cut the Duke of Arcester. The blood rushed to my face, a mist to my eyes. I stooped down and with my naked hands I seized one piece of that rock and with such strength as Hercules or Samson might have used, I drew it back, lifted it up and hurled it aside. The second piece followed in the same way. My mistress stood staring at me in awe mingled with terror. The way was opened and we stepped out upon the sand.

Never before or since did sunshine seem so sweet. My muddy clothes were torn to rags, blood was clotted in my hair and on my forehead, my face was black with sweat and dust, there were wounds upon my legs and arms. I was a gory and horrible spectacle. Mistress Lucy had suffered no wounds, but her clothes were rent and torn. Her face, too, was grimy, but beneath the dust and earth stain it showed as white as the cap of a wave.

"Thanks be to God," she said at last, "and you, we have won through."

I thought she would have fainted. I caught her by the arm, set her down upon the sand and sprinkled the water from the brook in her face until presently she revived.

"We are not safe yet," I urged. "There were hundreds of savages upon the island; they may not all have been at the cave. We must go warily, we cannot rest now."

"I am ready," she answered with great spirit, getting to her feet and stretching out her hand. "If you will help me I can go anywhere."

I still had my sword. I drew it out and led on, keeping well under the shelter of the cliffs. We walked up the sand toward the giant stairs. There we saw men, islanders, on the top of the wall, but my first glance told me that we had nothing to fear from them, for the stairs were gone. They were but a scattered heap of stones. The false gods were down, too. I wondered what had come to those at the main altar in the center of the island. The earthquake had crumbled the work of the builders of bygone years, and as the stairs had fallen away they had left the cliff sheer and bare for a hundred feet or more. Those above could not come at us, nor could we approach them, for which indeed we had no mind.

"It is an act of God," said I, "that has broken down the stairs."

"But there may be another way of descent," she said after a moment. "Oh, let us leave this dreadful island!"

I had no hope that the dinghy had been spared, but its place was not far away and we walked to it in silence. It was gone. A tidal wave had followed the earthquake. The canoes in which the islanders had come had been dashed to pieces and their few keepers killed. The survivors were prisoners on the island unless their friends came to their help, and even then, until they could devise some way of getting down the cliff. And we, too, were prisoners. Some of our gear, the compass, some provisions which I had stored in the crannies of the rock were still there, but they were useless to us. Something else had happened. The earthquake had broken the barrier reef. Before us was a practicable passage to the sea.

If we only had a boat! I turned to the canoes hopeful of finding one seaworthy, and as I did so my Mistress Lucy caught me by the arm.

"Look," she cried, pointing down the lagoon.

I turned and there, bottom upward, floated the dinghy. The sight of her was like a draught of wine. I turned and ran down the sand, followed by my lady. When opposite the boat I kicked off my shoes, I had on little else but shirt and trousers, jumped into the lagoon, swam to the dinghy and towed her ashore.

BOOK IV

ONCE MORE UPON THE SEAS

The Treasure Is Brought Home and All Is Well

CHAPTER XIX
WHEREIN WE CAPTURE THE SHIP

WE were so excited and exhausted by the terrific experiences which we had just gone through that a sort of frenzy possessed us. I know that word described my feelings and I think it also described my lady's feelings. We threw the things that we had saved, or that had escaped the earthquake and the tidal wave that followed it, into the boat pell-mell, climbed in ourselves, and shoved off. We could not get away from that island quick enough and we could not get far enough away once we started.

Luckily the oars had been secured to the thwarts, and I shipped them on the rowlocks forthwith, and then I rowed across the lagoon and through the opening in the reef. Indeed, the tidal wave had shattered the reef in various places and for the first time in centuries the sea made clean sweeps of the beach through the many openings. It was not altogether easy to row through the surf but it was child's play to our first passage over the reef. In spite of all that I had gone through, I felt as one possessed, and the stout ash oars fairly bent to my vigorous strokes. When we cleared the entrance, and got into smoother water, I shipped the oars, stepped the mast I had made during our sojourn on the island to take the place of the broken one, set a small sail I had improvised in idle moments out of some spare canvas which I had luckily found in the after locker together with the remaining pieces left over from my tailoring, and then I came aft and seized the tiller.

My lady had sat silent most of the time, closely watching me, but now she asked a pertinent question.

"Whither are we bound?"

Her interrogation recalled me to myself. I had really given the matter no thought at all. All that I had permitted myself to decide upon was to get away from the island, and I had hoisted the sail and put the boat before the wind without a thought as to its direction.

It so happened—indeed, I humbly submit that perhaps it did not happen by chance but was so ordered by that Providence which had watched over us—that the wind blew directly off the island and the boat was headed toward the distant shores of the other islands whence the marauders had come and where *The Rose of Devon* had been wrecked. I recollected from the conversation I had had with Pimball that they had somehow floated the ship and that she was seaworthy, and as my mistress questioned me the daring design of seizing the ship flashed into my mind.

Indeed, the enterprise was in a measure forced upon me. We had no water in the boat, practically no provisions. We were thousands of miles away from the possibility of passing ships. Unless some vessel should be blown far out of her course by continued storms there was absolutely no chance of our being picked up. That small boat with its patched-up, makeshift equipment was in no condition anyway for a long voyage, even if we had plenty of food and water. *The Rose of Devon* would provide everything we needed if we once got aboard her, and while two would be an almost impossible crew for such a ship, as I had said or thought, yet if any of her spars still stood, by means of tackles I might make shift to hoist a rag of sail. If the vessel were still tight she could carry us indefinitely, and perhaps by taking advantage of every wind that was favorable we might in the end make the South American Coast. Of course the work would all have to be done by me, but my lady had often steered *The Rose of Devon* during the outward voyage, for her pleasure, and she could relieve me long enough for me to get the absolutely necessary sleep so long as we were aboard her. At any rate, half-naked, hungry, thirsty, as we were in a small boat stripped of everything, she was our only resource. Therefore I answered briefly.

"I am going to seize *The Rose of Devon* if I can find her."

"But there will be men aboard her," said my mistress apprehensively.

"Doubtless," I returned, "but at most there cannot be many of them. We saw enough on the island to know that."

"Yes," admitted the brave woman by my side, "that is true."

"No one would offer to stay on the ship when he had a chance to hunt for treasure and for you and me."

"No, I suppose not."

"They would have to be constrained to stay there, and as I take it that the native fighting force of the island on which the ship was cast was in the canoes, there would not be any necessity for guarding her heavily. Besides, two or three with firearms could stop any attack that might be made."

"But we have no firearms," said my lady.

"We have weapons," I returned. I had picked up the musket from a shelf of rock where I had laid it, and she still clung to the pistol with which she had saved my life by her adroitness. "We have firearms," I continued, "but they are useless to us without powder and shot"— all that we had, had either been washed away or wetted so that it was of no use—"but I have my cutlass and I consider myself a match for all the murdering pirates that may be left on that ship."

"I believe that, too," she said, looking at me admiringly, "when I think of your determination, your feats of strength, your—"

"They were nothing. They did not measure up to the inspiration I had," said I.

But she shook her head at this and I continued, not daring to notice her overmuch.

"I take it that those islands are four or five leagues away," I looked over the side, "and this boat is making not more than three-quarters of a league an hour. That is all we can do with such a poor makeshift for a sail." I looked up into the sky, then at my watch. It was high noon. I had not dreamed that we had been so long in our adventures that day. "It will be dusk before we reach the nearest island. It may be that haply we shall find *The Rose of Devon* there."

"And if we do, what will be your plans?"

"I propose to douse the sail when we get near enough to see her, which will be long before she can see us, then wait until nightfall, take to the oars, row alongside, fasten the boat aft, and clamber aboard. If there are only two or three on her there will probably be but one on watch. I can throttle him without arousing the attention of the others. Perhaps I can confine the others below. Then we can cut the cable, hoist a rag of sail somehow, and be away before morning."

"But if there are savages aboard?"

"I do not think there will be any, but if there are I must even chance it."

"It sounds terribly dangerous."

"It is dangerous, but it is our only chance. How long do you think we would last in this open boat? In two or three days we would be mad for food and drink, burning up under this tropic sun."

"Could we not land on one of the other islands?"

"They are all populated, I take it, and our end would be certain."

"And what do you propose that I should do while you are fighting for me on the ship?"

"You will stay in the boat which I shall make fast to the ship, and if I should fail—"

"Oh, don't say that!"

"But I must say it. It is not beyond possibility that I shall, although I do not think it, because I believe God Who has preserved us hitherto does not intend that we shall finally fail. But if I should be overpowered or killed, there is a plug in the bottom of the boat. All you have to do is to cast off the painter and pull out the plug and—drift away."

The Island of the Stairs

"I understand," she said. "And if anything happens to you," she looked at me directly as she spoke, "I would rather drift away and drown—than live without you."

"Let us not dwell upon that," said I. "Let us hope that nothing will happen."

She nodded her head.

"Now," I continued, "I am going to ask you a strange thing."

She looked at me fearlessly and the trust and confidence of her next words repaid all my efforts a thousandfold.

"You can ask me anything you like," she said instantly.

"I am frightfully weary. I shall need what strength I have for the work of the night. The breeze is gentle and fair. There is no likelihood that it will change. All you have to do is to keep the boat on its course and awaken me if anything should change. Will you try it and help me thus far? I must have some sleep."

"I understand perfectly," was her brave and direct reply, "and you can go to sleep with perfect confidence. I will watch over you and the boat as best I can, God helping me. You know, I slept most of the night, myself, and I feel in no need of rest now."

With my cutlass I broke open a cocoanut, the milk and meat of which refreshed us both, and then, as I was, I threw myself down on the bottom of the boat, a hard bed, but one made soft by great weariness and want of sleep. The last thing I remember was the picture of Mistress Wilberforce, beautiful in her disarray, sitting in the stern sheets, holding the tiller in one hand and the sheet in the other, looking down upon me with a gaze I did not dare to think upon. I had no idea how weary I was, for I was asleep almost instantly, and it was five o'clock according to my watch before she awakened me with a touch of her little foot.

Although I was strained and stiff from the cramped position and the hard planking on which I lay, I knew that a stretch or two would fix me and I was greatly refreshed by my sleep and ready for a giant's work.

"I had to wake you," she said, reluctantly I thought, "because the island is in sight, and—"

"The ship!" I cried.

"Yes, you may see it dead ahead."

Whereat I got to my knees and shaded my eyes, for the sun had not yet set, and stared over the water.

Sure enough, there lay *The Rose of Devon*. She was still hull down in the shadow, but we could see the masts, that is, what was left of them. The mizzenmast was gone at the deck and the main topmast at the hounds, but the foremast still stood and the fore-topmast. The mainyard was still across, as were the two yards of the foremast. That was all I could make out then.

The island merited no particular description, for it was like hundreds of other South Seas Pacific islands. It was low and hilly and surrounded by a reef, but there was a broad opening through the reef, at least we thought so because the breakers suddenly ceased and there was a long stretch of smooth black water before they began again.

We had no time for many details, and indeed I came instantly to action. The breeze had practically died out and although the earthquake and tidal wave still caused a heavy sea, it was gradually quieting down to long, gentle undulations. I turned aft, unstepped the mast and doused the sail, carefully placing both where they might be of use in an emergency. Then I decided to let the boat drift for a while, until it grew dark enough to enable me to approach the ship without danger of observation.

We made a good meal off the scanty provisions we had left. My mistress was for saving them, but I bluntly pointed out that either we should have plenty in a few hours or be in no need of anything to eat forever after, so we satisfied our hunger and thirst abundantly, and then as it wanted an hour or two of night, I made my lady lie down, using the sail and my waistcoat to soften the planking, and rest in her turn. She obeyed me without question and, in spite of her declaration that she was not tired, I had the satisfaction of seeing in a few minutes that she had fallen asleep.

The Island of the Stairs

I sat silently watching her through the hours while the sun sank, while the dusk was followed by darkness, until the stars came out and then I stepped across her, seized the oars and started on my long pull toward the ship. We had drifted southward I opined, but I had taken my bearings carefully by the stars and I knew exactly in what direction to send the dinghy. The noise of the oars in the rowlocks finally awakened my lady. She got to her feet, went aft, took the tiller and, upon my giving her directions, steered a true course for the ship.

I suppose it was close on to nine o'clock when we reached her vicinity. I could not see my watch. We had no means of making a light, if we had dared upon the experiment. The night was dark and moonless and, save for the stars, as black as Egypt was fabled to be. The waves rolling through the opening of the reef and crashing on the shore drowned the noise of the oars in the rowlocks. The tide was in full flood, I judged, in fact just beginning to ebb, and the breeze which had sprung up after sunset was, as usual, offshore, two things greatly to our advantage.

We did not see the ship until we were almost upon her. Suddenly she loomed blackly out of the darkness, like a smudge of soot of darker hue than the rest. There was not a light upon her. I rowed close to her, rounded her counter, and discovered the Jacob's ladder which usually hung there still in place. I fastened the boat with a turn of the painter around the ladder and belayed it to a cleat aft, drew my sword from my sheath, and then turned for a last word.

"You know what to do if I don't come back?" I whispered.

She nodded. I put out my hand and she took it in both of hers. I was standing at the time and she was sitting, and before I could stop her she bent and kissed my great hand. I could not trust myself any further. With a prayer, silent but none the less fervent, I seized the rungs of the Jacob's ladder and slowly mounted to the level of the rail abaft the trunk cabin which served as a sort of poop deck. I had taken off my shoes before I did so, and save for the creaking caused by the swaying induced by my weight on the ladder, I went up without a sound.

I swung my leg over the rail, after having taken a quick look along the deck and having seen nothing. Before I disappeared over the side I turned and peered down through the blackness at her upturned face. I could see dimly its whiteness. I waved my hand to her and she waved hers in turn. She had the hardest part, that of sitting still, not knowing whether success was to attend our efforts or failure. The line that was attached to the boat plug was in her hand. The next few moments would determine whether she would rejoin me on the ship or whether she would cast off the painter, pull out the plug, and drift away with the young ebb.

I had that picture in my mind's eye, too, and if I had needed anything to nerve me to the service of my mistress it would have been that. I had carried my cutlass in my teeth as I climbed up the ladder. I instantly shifted it to my hand, peering carefully about me as I made my way along the top of the cabin. The deck was in a frightful state of confusion. One of the deck houses had been blown in by the storm and pieces of wreckage lay all about. The starboard rail had been shattered along the waist. They had made little effort it seemed to clear up the raffle and the wreckage.

I made my way forward slowly and with all the softness of a great cat until I came to the break of the cabin. Everything was in shadow and darkness, of course, yet I thought I detected someone leaning against the starboard rail on the quarter-deck abreast the mainmast, looking toward the land. I stared and the longer I stared the more convinced I became that someone was there. I crossed over to the port side and slipped down to the quarter-deck. Silently as before, I made my way over the littered deck in the direction of the standing figure.

If the deck had been clear, I could have reached him without attracting his attention, but within a few feet of him I stepped upon a round marlinspike which slid under my feet and the effort to recover my balance aroused the watcher's attention. He looked around suspiciously, but the next moment I was upon him. I did not know how many people were on that ship and I could not afford to make any noise. If I were to succeed I must deal with the enemy one at a time. I caught this man by the throat with one hand. The next instant

I saw a flash of something in the air and I was just in time to seize his descending arm grasping his sheath knife.

I held him in an iron grip. He kicked at me viciously but I lifted him higher into the air and sank my fingers tighter and tighter in his throat. Thereafter I held him there waiting. God knows how I accomplished it, but I did. Presently I felt him grow limp in my hands. I had broken his wrist I discovered afterward, and had nearly choked him to death. I laid him down on the deck and with a piece of rope I lashed him hand and foot. I didn't know whether he was dead or not but I couldn't afford to take any chances. I doubled another piece of rope and thrust it tightly between his jaws which I pried open, and so left him bound and gagged.

I thought I had worked silently, but either I had made more noise than I fancied or else it had come time for them to relieve the watch. But for whatsoever cause it may be, as I was bending over him, a ray of light suddenly shot through the darkness. It came from the companion hatchway which opened on the deck from the low break of the trunk cabin, rising a few feet above the quarter-deck. I sprang to my feet and turned instantly, sword in hand, and the next instant three figures broke out of the light. The lantern they carried illuminated me completely. If I had had more time I should have jumped back into the shadows—I was quick-witted enough to think of it—but the time was lacking.

The next moment the three precipitated themselves upon me. They were half dressed, two of them had sheath knives and the third a cutlass. Fortunately none of them had brought a pistol. They were courageous enough, I will say that for them. And his daring brought the first man who had the drawn sword to his fate, for as he lunged at me I spitted him with my own cutlass. I drove the blow home to the hilt. The man went down like a ninepin, dragging the sword from my hand, and as fortune would have it he fell in front of number two, staggering him so that he dropped the lantern, leaving the deck in darkness save for the light which came from the after cabin. Being otherwise weaponless, I received number two with a mighty blow on the jaw from my clenched fist which temporarily accounted for him. Number three wavered indecisively for a moment giving me time to draw out my cutlass from the body of the dead man. The blade was broken off about six inches from the point, but nevertheless in a hand like mine it was a terrible weapon. I did not give him time to recover, for I sprang upon him. He thrust at me with his own knife half-heartedly, but in a moment I struck it out of his hand and sent it flying over the rail and into the sea.

"Now," said I, "get down on your knees and beg for your life."

There must have been something compelling in my manner for he instantly obeyed me. He threw himself flat before me and it was not until I prodded him with my blade that he stopped howling.

"Tell me quickly," I said, "and tell me truly, who are on the ship?"

"There were four of us," he began.

"That is enough for the present," I answered, for I had accounted for the whole four. "Any natives?"

"None."

"Come with me," I said.

I caught him by the collar of his shirt, dragged him to his feet, marched him along the deck, and bundled him to the forepeak. I drew the hatch cover, battened it down and locked it. I knew that he could not get out until I let him. Then I walked back to the man I had struck with my fist but discovered no signs of returning consciousness in him. He was still helpless but I lashed and gagged him as I had the first man. Having made sure that I had nothing to fear from these men I sprang to the rail on the top of the trunk cabin.

"Mistress Lucy," I cried.

"Oh, thank God, thank God," came her voice in the darkness. "I heard the shouting, I saw the light. Are you unharmed?"

"Entirely," I answered, "and I have the ship. Leave the boat fast as it is and climb aboard. Stay, perhaps I would better descend and help you."

"No," she said, "I can manage it myself."

I leaned far over the rail and as soon as she came within reach I caught her arm and presently I had the satisfaction of lifting her up on the top of the trunk cabin by my side.

The Island of the Stairs

"Safe now!" I cried triumphantly, resisting an overwhelming temptation to take her in my arms and shout for joy.

"What next?" she asked.

Singular how she asked me that question in every emergency. Well, I had, as I generally had, an answer for her.

"I will get another lantern out of the cabin," I answered, "and then we shall see."

To leap down the companion ladder and fetch the lantern burning there was the work of a few seconds. I had forgot the dead man whom I had thrust through with my sword, but there he lay in full view. My mistress screamed faintly. I cursed myself for my forgetfulness. I had her turn her back and without more ado I picked the dead man up and hurled him overboard, praying that God might have mercy on his soul, but otherwise giving him little thought.

"Here are two men," said I, flashing the lantern over them, "they are still alive but bound and helpless. I must get the ship under way and I must depend upon you. If you will come forward with me we will make shift to hoist the jib or staysail, it is all we can do in this darkness. We will cut the cable, and as the wind is offshore and the tide beginning to ebb, we will get away from these horrible islands."

Hand in hand we ran rapidly forward. Fortunately, the bowsprit still stood, even the flying jib boom was in place. I overhauled the gear and the two of us hoisted the jib, my lady pulling on the halyards with me like a little man.

"Now," said I, "do you go aft and take the wheel. Take the lantern with you. I will hold out the jib sheet, cast her head to port, and tell you in what direction to steer."

She hesitated a moment, fearful at leaving me.

"There is no danger," I said. "There were but four men on the ship, one is dead and overboard, another locked up in the forepeak beneath my feet, and two are as helpless as logs."

"I will go," said the girl resolutely, "although it is frightfully dark."

"The least call will bring me to your side," said I. "Take the lantern with you. I need it not."

I watched her walk rapidly along the deck, lantern in hand. When she reached the wheel I told her to cast off its lashings, put it amidships, and then with an axe, which I had found lying where they had left it after they had cut the wreckage of the masts away, I severed the cable. Thereafter I called aft to my lady to put the helm hard astarboard. The bow of *The Rose of Devon* slowly swung around, the sail filled and presently I had the satisfaction of seeing her slip through the entrance in the lagoon, past the reef and into the open sea.

I belayed the jib sheet, ran aft and took the helm. We were free. My mistress refused to go below, refused to leave my side in fact, so until daybreak we remained on deck, I steering, she seated close by. And so we sped on through the sweet summer night.

CHAPTER XX
SHOWS HOW WE SAILED TO SAFETY AGAIN

I DO not suppose that a man and a woman were ever confronted with a greater task than that which we faced that morning. The problem met me in so many ways that I was fairly puzzled at it. The two men lying bound and gagged on the deck had, of course, recovered consciousness. The man below in the forepeak had given some noisy signs of his presence. These three had to be dealt with in some way. The ship itself was wrecked, aloft that is, and I had as yet no means of telling whether she were tight below, although, as I deemed she sat about as usual in the water, I concluded that if she had sprung a leak they had succeeded in stopping it.

The dawn disclosed a white-faced man and woman staring at each other near the wheel. Breakfast was a problem in itself, too. On the one hand, I did not like to send my lady below without at least having made some sort of inspection myself, nor did I like to leave her alone on deck, on the other.

"Of what are you thinking?" she asked presently, seeing my brows knitted with the stress of my mental effort.

"Breakfast, first of all, something to eat."

"Let me go below and get it."

"No," I replied, "I must see what's below first myself."

"Very well then," was her prompt, brave answer. She rose as she spoke and seized the spokes of the wheel. "I will steer the ship, only do you hurry back."

"If I only had a pistol to leave with you," I said.

"There is no danger," she answered bravely enough, "there were only four men on the ship you said. One is dead, one is locked up forward, and the other two—"

"I will make sure about them," I interrupted, going over and examining the lashings of the two.

They were frightened to death and the man with the broken wrist, although I didn't know it then, was suffering greatly. Their eyes were mutely appealing, but I had no pity to waste. Seeing that they were tightly bound and the hatch forward securely battened, I turned and ran below.

As fortune would have it a brace of pistols lay on the table in the cabin. One of them was loaded and primed and ready for use. It was lucky for me that they had not used it last night, I thought. I snatched it up, returned to the deck, and laid it at my lady's side. Thereafter I felt much safer for I knew she could use it on occasion. I then went below and resumed my search. The cabin was frightfully untidy and disorderly. Some of the mutineers at least had made it their headquarters and the table was covered with an accumulation of soiled dishes. On a platter I found some cold salt beef and bread and other things. There was no time to be dainty, but I did make shift to clean a plate, heaped it with hard bread and beef, drew a pannikin of water, and returned to the deck with it. We made our first breakfast by the wheel.

I had been thinking hard and I had come to the conclusion that our only safety lay in keeping the three members of the crew securely locked up. If I could have depended upon one of them the problem would have been simplified immensely, and if I could have depended upon two we could have got along with some degree of comfort, for the three of us with the aid of tackles could have handled the ship while my lady steered. But it was not to be thought of.

First I took the gags out of the mouths of the two men, whereat he of the broken wrist told me of his hurt. I cast off the lashings to verify his statement. I had brought up from my cabin and from Captain Matthews' several sets of irons for wrists and ankles. They had not disturbed them although they had otherwise rummaged and plundered the cabins and had destroyed much in them wantonly. I clapped double irons on the villain who was unhurt and irons on the ankles of the man with the broken wrist. He was in great pain and more or less helpless. I fastened his feet to a ring bolt in the deck and then took the other man and stowed him below in my cabin which I carefully cleared of everything and which I securely locked on the outside. He was a small, slight man and I knew that the door would hold him, but to make assurance doubly sure, I intended to put up a bar when I had time.

Him of the broken wrist I put in the fourth cabin which had not been occupied during the cruise, as we had carried no second mate. Before I turned the lock on him I set his wrist and put it in splints as best I could. It was his right wrist and little danger could be expected from him. Nevertheless, I locked him up securely. I saw that each room was provided with bread and meat and water. I told them that I would visit them once a day and give them food enough for the day, and that if they attempted to break out I would give them short shrift indeed.

Taking the pistol from my mistress, I then went forward, opened the fore hatch and descended into the forepeak. It was well I had a weapon, for the man had possessed himself of a cutlass and I have no doubt, if I had not presented the pistol at him so soon as I put foot on the ladder, he would have cut me down. I had some trouble in getting him to put down his weapon, he was so ugly and disobedient, and I had about made up my mind to pull the trigger and end it, as I had no time to waste on a murderer like that one. I guess he must have seen in my face that my patience was at an end for finally I had him in double irons as well. I left him in the forecastle, first making a thorough search for and removing everything that he would be able to use as a weapon. A good many of the seamen's chests were there but they were locked and I didn't disturb them, as he had no means of getting into them. I told him what I had told the others. He was the biggest and strongest man and he had the strongest prison. The forepeak was separated from the rest of the ship by a stout bulkhead and the only way he could get out was by the hatch, which I drew over until it was but six inches open and there I secured it. The first part of the problem was thus solved.

During all this, my mistress had stood bravely by the helm. I shall never forget how beautiful she looked, with the fresh breeze bringing color into her pale cheeks and blowing back wisps of her golden hair, lovely in its disarray. We were both of us exactly as we had been when we came out of the cave. I was about to go on further business when she interrupted me.

"If you please," she began with unusual humility, "Master Hampdon, if you can spare me a little while to myself now I should like to go below. Perhaps the villains have left some of my clothes intact and I may change my dress and wash my face, and —"

"I am a brute not to have thought of it," I said. "Keep the pistol with you. Who knows what may chance? I will take the wheel. Come to me as soon as you may, for I shall be anxious when you are out of my sight. When I have finished on the deck I expect to make a thorough investigation of the ship to see what condition she is in and what is best to be done."

"I shall hasten," she said, turning away and tripping lightly down the ladder.

In an incredibly short time she was back transformed. Although her cabin had been occupied by some of the men and her things had been overhauled and were in a state of confusion, yet she had found suitable clothing and she presently came up on deck looking as fresh and dainty as if she had never been on an adventure in her life. And yet, will you believe me? it was with a certain very vivid regret I saw her put aside the tunic I had made her, which had served her so well.

"I suppose," said I, "that I ought to be doing the same thing, but there will be time enough for that later on. How do you feel?"

"Fit for anything."

"And you will take the wheel?"

"Gladly."

"Very well," said I, "you have nothing to do but keep her before the wind."

With that, axe in hand I went forward. I put in the hardest hour or two of work in my life. I never stopped a moment except to throw back a word or two to my little mistress guiding the ship. By the time I had finished, the decks of *The Rose of Devon* presented an entirely different appearance. I had chopped away and thrown overboard the mast wreckage. When it was too heavy, I clapped a tackle to it to assist me. The tangled gear had been overhauled and each brace, line, and halyard had been coiled and hung to its proper pin. Although the ship looked desolate and forlorn enough to a sailor, and to anyone else perhaps, there was no confusion or disorder.

By this time it was high noon. I knocked off work therefore and, upon her insistence, relieved her at the wheel while she went below to the lazarette where the cabin stores were kept, to prepare us something to eat. She said that was her task, and although it irked me to see her compelled to do anything, there was truth in her words. I can do most things but cook. There, I confess, I fail. I did kindle a fire for her in the galley, however, and about one o'clock we had a royal dinner, the first civilized meal, so to speak, that we had enjoyed since the day of the mutiny. She brought it up on deck and we ate it together. After dinner she surprised me by proffering me a pipe which she had found below—it had been Captain Matthews'—and a pouch of tobacco, and nothing would do but that I must smoke before turning to again. I confess that it tasted sweet to me, and felt sorry that she could not enjoy the luxury, and told her so, which seemed to give her great amusement.

Her light-heartedness cheered me immensely. To be sure she did not quite imagine the extent of the problem that lay before us, or perhaps she knew more about it than I fancied, but whatever be the facts, I could not feel downhearted or downcast when she smiled at me as she did then.

Well, the hour of refreshment and rest at last came to an end. Surrendering the wheel to her, I went forward. I had determined to loose the mainsail first, if I could, and then loose the foresail and topsail. The first was an easy enough task. It took me some time to climb out on each of the yardarms and cast off the gaskets, but presently the huge sail hung in the buntlines. I came down by the backstays, clapped a watch tackle on each sheet and finally succeeded in getting the sail set as taut as the bolt ropes would allow. My mistress clapped her hands with joy when I had succeeded. The slow pace of the ship was much increased by the draw of the big mainsail.

I did the same thing with the foresail and then boldly tackled the fore-topsail, but here I met with greater difficulties for the topsail yard—it was a single topsail—had to be mastheaded if the sail was to be of any use. Although I clapped several tackles on it and pulled and hauled lustily, it taxed my strength beyond its limit. It was my mistress who came to my assistance. She lashed the wheel amidships while watching me pull at the halyards, and came and seized the tarred rope with her own hands and laid back with a will.

It was just the added pound or two that was needed, and slowly, readjusting the tackles from time to time, we at last mastheaded the fore-topsail yard. I was glad that *The Rose of Devon* was a small ship, for had that yard been a foot longer or a pound heavier, we had never done it. When I had finished I carefully braced the yards, then I cast off the lashings of the wheel and shifted it until the wind came from the starboard quarter and lo and behold we were headed due eastward!

The breeze was growing stronger but it was still gentle. It blew fair and held steady. If it would only blow long enough and hold without change we would inevitably fetch the South American coast, which I estimated something more than fifteen hundred leagues away.

I rested a while but not for long. It was late in the afternoon, yet I felt it necessary further to overhaul the ship; so leaving my mistress again in charge, a solitary woman on a half wrecked ship in a great waste of unknown seas!—I tell you this that you may see how brave she was—I went below, having first sounded the well and found to my joy that there was no more than the usual amount of water in it and that the ship evidently was tight. She must have gone on the sand in the storm in such a way as not to start a leak, although it might be that a plank had been started and that the men aboard her, one of whom was an expert carpenter, had been able to get at it and caulk it up. At any rate, she was tight.

Everything below was in a state of disorder but no especial damage had been done. I cleaned out the cabin, washed the dishes and made everything snug. In the cabin that Pimball had occupied after my departure I found the famous chart and the little image, both of which I put carefully away. I was glad to see them again. We have them still and often show them to our children and friends as we tell again this tale.

The Island of the Stairs

I also estimated the provisions in the lazarette. There was plenty of food for our immediate needs, although most of the liquor was gone. Then I went down into the hold. I found enough supplies there to last the five of us who were on board indefinitely. The arms chest had been broken open and most of the arms were gone—I suspected that they were back on the Island of the Stairs! Those that remained I carefully removed, and finding powder and shot, I charged them and placed them under lock and key in Captain Matthews' cabin, which I had reserved for my own use.

By the time I had finished, night had almost fallen. I stopped before the doors where I had confined the prisoners and asked them how they did and if they wanted anything, being met with oaths and curses from one man and cries of pain from the other, to which I was alike indifferent. I also visited the man in the forecastle and then came back to take the wheel while my lady got our supper.

I don't think I was ever so tired in my life. As I look back upon it it seems to me that I had done ten men's work. And yet there was nothing but thankfulness in my heart as I hung over the spokes and watched the ship rush toward safety through the gently rolling seas. How mercifully God had protected us. How He had used me to keep harm from this poor, helpless young woman. I thanked Him for all His kindness and prayed for a continuance of that favor until we got safely home.

Supper was soon ready and it was a fine one. My shipmate's skill at cookery surprised me. She had not stinted in her preparations, and the best that the ship afforded, and I have told you that she was expensively, even luxuriously, stocked, was spread before me. How I did eat! I am ashamed to think on it, even to this day. After supper I had another pipe, and then plans for the night had to be adjusted.

"Do you go below, Mistress Lucy," I said, "and turn in. I have my watch and I will awaken you at midnight. You can then take the wheel, and—"

"No," said the girl, "I can't think of going below where those men are confined. It is balmy out here. I shall sleep here on the deck at your feet, within touch and call. I'd rather have it so."

The Island of the Stairs

I sought to change her decision but, as in all matters which were not really vital, I was more or less helpless.

"Well," said I, "since you are resolved, take the wheel and I will bring up your things to make you comfortable."

With that I descended to her cabin and brought up a mattress, pillow, and blankets, which I laid on the deck. The sea had gone down and the ship was steady so my lady could lie comfortably without being cast against anything, but for precaution's sake I put the mattress against the foot of the trunk cabin in the angle formed by the companionway. Before Mistress Lucy went to sleep we had our evening prayers. I had lighted the binnacle lamp in order to see the compass course and she stood by it, reading a psalm from her prayer book, which she had carried ever with her, and so on until we said good-night. She lay down at once and closed her eyes and I thought she was asleep.

The steering of the ship was not very exhausting. Under the diminished sail, which was all that we could carry, she steered easily and the wheel did not make many demands upon me. I confess frankly that I never was so utterly weary in my life. I had not had a regular sleep for three days and I had worked to the extreme limit of my strength during all that time. I found myself nodding over the wheel and finally I must have gone sound asleep. The pressure of my body as I leaned on the spokes brought the ship around and it was the tremendous slatting of the sails in the wind, which was ever freshening, that awoke me.

The noise awoke my mistress too. She had learned the sailor's trick of waking with all her faculties at her command, and this time she realized the situation and came to her senses quicker than I did.

"You were asleep," she said, rising.

"Aye, that I was," I answered shamefacedly, bringing the ship before the wind again.

"What time is it?" she asked.

When the sails began to draw once more, I pulled out my watch and soon discovered that it was only nine o'clock.

"I have had one hour's sleep," she said, "and am able to take the watch now. I should not have taken advantage of your offer before. You have done enough in the past three days to have killed half a dozen ordinary men. Now, do you go to sleep and I will watch."

"You will wake me at midnight?" I asked.

She nodded. At this I put my watch into her hand and started to go below.

"No," she said, "you must not leave me. Go to sleep here on the deck where I can call you if necessary."

I tumbled down on the mattress I had fixed for her and almost before I could draw the blanket over me I was asleep. I say it to my shame and her glory that she let me sleep the long night through, for it was the sunlight that awakened me, and when I opened my eyes, there she stood, erect and dauntless, matchless, holding the wheel.

CHAPTER XXI
AND LOVE ROUNDS OUT THE TALE

THERE is little more to tell. One day was like another. For once that ocean which I had always thought ill-called Pacific, did not belie its name. The wind blew us steadily and gently toward the haven we wished to reach. It was hard work but we equally divided watches and duties, I attending to all the trimming of the yards, my mistress doing the cooking, and after that first night we honorably kept watch and watch at night. I do not know what would have happened if it had come on to blow, for I never could have reefed or furled those sails, but the same Providence which had watched over us kept us in recollection still. Indeed, save for a certain nervous strain, I was never better in my life, and my mistress also.

After many days' sailing we approached the South American coast and there were lucky enough to fall in with a Spanish frigate. Her commander, Don Antonio Recaldé, came aboard when he heard from the officer whom he had sent off to us something of our story. He was incredulous at first and not until we showed him some of the jewels did he believe us. There was a great risk, perhaps, in showing an ordinary man such a valuable treasure, but we were both agreed, my lady and I, that Don Antonio was to be trusted absolutely.

Indeed, he proved himself a royal fellow in that he took the three mutineers on his own ship and sent a lieutenant and a dozen seamen aboard *The Rose of Devon*, and as he was cruising on a roving commission he convoyed us into Valparaiso. The prisoners we turned over to the English representative, to be tried for piracy and murder. A trading ship bound through the Straits of Magellan for Buenos Ayres offered us an opportunity to return to the Atlantic. We took advantage of this, disposing of *The Rose of Devon* to a firm of Spanish merchants at Valparaiso for a good price which provided us with more than enough money for our return voyage, and which relieved us of the necessity for offering some of the jewels for sale which would have involved explanations and possibly delay and confiscation.

The Island of the Stairs

We did press upon Don Antonio an emerald of great size and brilliancy which, generous seaman that he was, he was loath to take but which my mistress insisted upon, in addition to which he received a certain percentage of the proceeds of the sale of *The Rose of Devon* as salvage, so that he and his men were well rewarded for their kindness to us.

From Buenos Ayres, which we reached without mishap, we took a coasting vessel, the only one that served, for Rio de Janeiro, the capital of the Portuguese possessions in the Brazils. There we were lucky enough to find a large Portuguese man-of-war frigate homeward bound to Lisbon, whose captain obligingly received us as passengers, being moved thereto, I more than suspect, by the beauty of my lady. From Lisbon by roundabout ways we finally landed in Plymouth Harbor, whence we had set forth more than a twelvemonth before. How good it was to set foot on English ground once more! Yet I was sadder that morning than I had been during all our far voyaging. I hired a private coach and by nightfall we ended all our long journey at Master Ficklin's door. He, with that worthy kindly woman his sister, greeted us as if we had risen from the dead, and greatly rejoicing in my lady's good fortune, gave us the warmest of welcomes.

That night I had what I expected would be my last interview with her. We had been thrown constantly together during the six months that had elapsed since our great adventure on the Island of the Stairs and our arrival in England. We had discussed everything else, I think, but I had said naught of my love. Indeed, each league of sea over which we passed on our way homeward seemed to remove her farther from me. Although she was tender, she was considerate, she was inviting, she was intimate, when she was not arch, I could not bring myself to a declaration.

We were alone. Good Mistress Ficklin had given us her parlor for the evening. I took from my pockets the canvas pouch filled with her treasure which I had detached from my belt as I had dressed that morning, and laid it on the table.

"This, Mistress Wilberforce," said I, formally enough, although my heart was beating rapidly, "is yours."

The Island of the Stairs

She waved her hand as if it was of small moment.

"We have discussed that before," she said, "what of yourself?"

"Last night," I replied, "I went down to the docks. A ship sails for the East Indies next week. They want a chief mate and if my references serve they will engage me."

"And have you these references?"

"I thought, madam, that your friends in the city might give them to me when they know."

"But I have no friends in the city," she answered promptly.

"These," said I, pointing to the table, "will buy them for you."

She stepped over to the table, untied the strings and upon the velvet cloth fell the sparkling gems.

"Would they not buy friends for you as well?" she asked.

"Mistress Lucy," said I, "I want but one thing in this world. No money, no jewels could buy that, nor all the treasure we left behind upon that island."

"But if one should give you that," she said very softly, her eyes on the table and her white hand lifting the stones and letting them fall.

"I am not worthy—to receive it," said I.

"And so," she said, without looking at me, "and so it is good-by then. May you be happy."

She extended her hand to me and I caught it and kissed it passionately, but when I made to let it go she would not.

"Master Hampdon," she said, looking at me, her eyes brighter than the diamonds and bluer than the sapphires upon the table, "you are a fool."

"Right well I know that, Mistress," said I, striving to fetch a smile to match her own.

"And a blind man as well."

Whereat I was a blind man, indeed, for my eyes misted up, but not with blood as in the battle. And I, as strong and tough as a mountain ash, was as like to faint as any lovesick girl.

"John, John," came the sweetest voice on earth to me through the darkness, "don't you see? Don't you know that I love you and you only, that you have all my heart and that my life, which is yours a thousand times on sea and shore, is not worth living without you?"

"But your friends, your world," I protested as she came nearer.

"I have no other friends, I want no other, and you are my world."

Well, it was not in me to resist after that, and for the third time in my life I held her in my arms, where since that hour she has often been again, and for the third time I drank the sweetness of her lips. She laughed presently and I let her go a little, yet still held her close, and she looked at me.

"Do you remember the night on *The Rose of Devon* when first you kissed me?"

"If I should kiss you a million times, sweetheart, as I mean to do," I answered boldly, "I should not forget a single one of them, much less that."

"And to punish you for your presumption, although my heart went out to you I do confess, I struck you; and to teach you to be a dutiful husband, loving, devoted to me," she paused and laughed again, "I strike you once again."

Whereat she laid her hand once more, but in tenderness, upon my cheek, following it with a kiss. I have had his Majesty's sword laid upon my shoulder after I had led one of the King's ships to victory in the French wars, and I am now, if you please, Sir John Hampdon. We live at Wilberforce Castle and our children play on the sward, but the royal accolade meant not so much to me as that light blow upon my cheek with which my dear mistress sealed our plighted troth.

Note

I am often asked what became of the surviving English on the island, and I can only answer that I do not know. So far as I have learned, no white man has ever visited that island since that day, although the publication of these memoirs may induce someone to go there for the balance of the treasure, which is undoubtedly still where we left it. They were resourceful sailors, however, and I have no doubt if any of them survived the earthquake, they managed to get down the wall in some way, repaired their canoes perhaps and returned to the island whence they came, with the surviving natives, and they and their descendants may be living there, awaiting the arrival of some ship.

I heard also after some years, of the prisoners we left in the hands of the British representative at Valparaiso. One died, one escaped, and one was hanged for the mutiny. Should anyone be inspired by the recital of this story to seek the Island of the Stairs—where what remains of the treasure is theirs for the taking—and come upon these mutineers, they may assure them that, so far as my lady and I are concerned, no proceedings will be instituted against them. The lapse of years and the punishment their ringleaders suffered have rendered any prosecution of them impossible, and so far as we are concerned they may return to England or go where they will without molestation. God has undoubtedly dealt with them, and we can leave their future to Him.

JOHN HAMPDON, KT.

THE END

Copyright © 2023 Esprios Digital Publishing. All Rights Reserved.